Lockdown + 3 Alphas = Heat: An Omega's Thrilling Dark Romantic Adventure

Lori Laidlaw

Published by Lynda French, 2024.

This is a work of fiction. Similarities to real people, places, or events are entirely coincidental.

LOCKDOWN + 3 ALPHAS = HEAT: AN OMEGA'S THRILLING DARK ROMANTIC ADVENTURE

First edition. January 25, 2024.

Written by Lori Laidlaw.

To all the lovers who want to see just how red that flag can get!

Part One

Fuck. My. Life.

Tonight's the biggest party of the DECADE and I can't go. Why? Because three Alpha-holes have booked this crummy private club for the evening and I have to stay and serve them. Wearing a stupid costume that doesn't even fit right.

Why? Because the real hostesses get to go to the County Decennial Celebration taking place in Vista Valley so oh hey, guess who is suddenly good enough to do a servers job?

This is such bullshit. I'll be too old to really enjoy myself by time the next Decennial party rolls around. I'll be like.. thirty.

Both Mandy and Marcie practically laughed themselves sick at me being stuck behind. They're almost mirror images of each other: tall, one golden-blonde the other strawberry-blonde, natural C cups, legs that go on forever, but that old saying about beauty only being skin-deep might have been written for them. They're nasty, spiteful, hateful girls who like to push me around.

Then there's me, Lake, although no one actually calls me by my name. I'm skinny, have white-blonde hair, barely an A cup bra size, and scrawny legs. I look like a cross between a starving ghost and a gawky, consumptive child. Mandy calls me Puddle and the nickname has stuck. I guess I should be thankful no one's thought of Mud Puddle.

I do all the drudge work at this A-list Gentlemens Club called, with great originality, the A-list Gentlemens Club. I guess having the same slogan and business name saves a lot on advertising. I think it's stupid but, to be fair, today everything feels stupid. Especially me.

I called it a crummy club but truth is it's really nice. A red-brick building with white window sills and shutters, and lots of green ivy, that turns pretty shades of red in the Fall, climbing the walls. It looks good, but I'm not a fan of the bees it attracts.

The floors are all ceramic tile or marble, and there are lots of thick Persian rugs and runners. Plenty of pictures on the walls with heavy-looking ornate frames in gold. They're all of naked women but since they're oil paintings instead of photos I guess that makes them art instead of porn.

It's a man's club – supposedly for gentlemen – so the big, heavy furniture is made of dark wood and leather in burgundy and forest green. It smells good with the lingering smoke from expensive cigars and high-priced aftershave and cologne.

I'm strictly back-of-house meaning washing dishes then bussing dishes so I can wash some more. The kitchen is crap. Well, I guess it's good for the chef, he's got all the fancy chrome stuff, but the floors here are linoleum, all cracked so you know that means they're really old and hard to clean, and the counters are formica. I didn't know the names of these things until I heard the staff complaining that we're probably all inhaling asbestos.

All the money gets spent on the members areas and nothing on improving the working conditions back here. These back rooms also have florescent lighting which has an unpleasant hum. No wonder I'm so pale, always stuck in the far corner of the kitchen.

I'm twenty years old but I look about fourteen because I'm a runt. I get picked on and bullied, taken for granted and used. Although I'm a wolf-shifter I spent my childhood as a human having been a rescued foundling infant. Raised in an orphanage I was able to go to school where I discovered an affinity with numbers and a love of reading: quiet non-physical activities.

It also meant I was taught nothing about my wolf nature, a side of me I didn't even know existed until at age sixteen, late from undernourishment, I hit puberty. Like a truck slamming full-speed into a brick wall. Adolescent angst pales compared to adolescent wolf angst.

Raging hormones turned me from an unloved and miserable wimp into a vicious temperamental fighter. The first time I shifted was involuntary and I thought I'd been bitten by a werewolf unawares. As if that could happen, wolf bites hurt plenty!

I got kicked out of the home and had to live off the streets – the same fate my own kind had abandoned me to all those years before: to starve in the street like a mutt. That's where I met some other shifters, not all of them wolves, and learned a little about who and what I was.

But I was leery of strangers, afraid of everyone, or at least unable to trust anyone. Fear turned me into a scrapper but my too-small size meant I lost most fights.

Shifting was a difficult and painful process at first but I practiced and practiced and eventually got it down pat. Unfortunately city streets are no place for a wolf. Since cis-humans attack what frightens them the safest places I could find were in derelict, sparsely populated areas. That's how I found the alleyway behind The Gentlemens Club and eventually wormed my way inside as a menial worker.

No one there knows I can shift, but when the mean hostesses bully me sometimes it's really hard to keep my wolf nature in check. But, for overall survival, I need to keep that truth hidden by keeping my head down.

I'm certainly the most unthreatening-looking person ever! Inadequate feeding has left me with zero resistance so I catch every germ around and am usually sniffling or sneezing. When my nose isn't red I have no color at all.

Well, okay I do have the most amazing eyes. When I look in the mirror I even shock myself. It was a teacher, way back when, who first called them aquamarine and she taught me how to spell the word. It's the only exotic-sounding thing about me.

Okay, enough of the pity-party, right? I'd rather be angry than mopey. And I have good reason, too. I mean, they NEVER, EVER let me serve in the Club, especially when there are visiting VIPs, but yeah when everybody else wants to go to the big party well then it's a different story. Suddenly it's *oh sure, Puddle can take care of the VIPs.*

I was already cranky and this has really pissed me off. Especially since these guests are wolves, too. I've had very little interaction with fellow shifters and I've always avoided Alphas: aggressive, domineering, intimidating males. Ugh!

Milán, the Club Manager who might even be the owner because that's a bit of a mystery, must not care too much about these Alpha-holes to stick them with me, though. Of course I think they're pond-scum to insist on a private function in the Club tonight of all nights. Maybe Milán has just said *sorry, but she's the best I can do, everyone else has booked off.*

I won't be talking to the Alpha-holes because they don't speak English and I don't speak anything else. I guess we'll be playing charades! Actually it won't be too bad because they didn't show up here until eleven, after dinner anyways, so I just have to serve drinks and some snack food. They each arrived separately and with an interval between.

All very hush-hush. They want privacy so hopefully they'll be happy if I bring out a selection of bottles and let them serve themselves.

That would be best for me because my crankiness isn't just at missing out on the party of the decade, no, it's also hormonal. I'm in pre-heat. I should be okay for at least one more day, I'm not lubricating yet, but even if these men are Alpha-holes they're still Alphas and that scares me. If my scent turns really sweet I'm afraid I'll trigger them to rut. One coming after me will be bad enough but three? They'll fight each other and tear me apart in the process.

I'm calling them #1, #2, and #3 but of course they do have names. First is Sandor and I call him #1 because he's the oldest. Second – #2 – is Janos the chatty one, and #3 is called Antal-the-Gorgeous.

Despite everything I have to admit these are three hunky men who look like they stepped off the pages of GQ magazine. The Eastern European edition. Especially Antal. He truly looks like a male model if the ad is for what the well-dressed hired killer is wearing this season. Including tattoos on the back of his hands, and probably everywhere else, too.

And not those cheap jail tattoos of L-O-V-E and H-A-T-E across his knuckles, oh no, these are a swirling pattern of skulls and roses and trailing ivy and twisting snakes. My eyes want to follow them up his arms.

They're all dressed in expensive well-tailored suits that can't disguise their muscular physiques under what looks like very pricey cloth. Their weapons are well-hidden, though. Nobody has a paunch, and neatly trimmed beards hide any double-chins. The tidy barbering extends to hair cut stylishly short.

Oh great, Milán, speaking in their own language, has just introduced me and now they're all having a laugh. The Alpha-holes glance my way with amusement and I'm not impressed. I don't care that their smiles show off healthy white teeth and handsome faces that crinkle round the eyes, eyes that seem to have a very penetrating focus.

I'm sure I've got a sullen, sulky expression but that just seems to entertain them. Milán turns to me saying they think my name is a joke and they're going to call me *Tó* which is Lake in Hungarian, but only because *Tócsa,* meaning Puddle, is too long.

Bunch of freakin' comedians.

So they're Hungarian. That's where the gypsies come from, right? I thought that ethnic group were short-statured with dark hair and dark complexions – well, except for the vampires, that is – but these men are sandy or fair-haired and tall and big. Of course since I have to take a deep breath to measure five feet high everyone looks big and tall to me.

A fourth man, Kartal, came in with them and he's somebody's Beta but I didn't pay much attention so I don't know whose. He speaks English and can translate but he didn't stay long. Apparently Kartal will be waiting outside with the vehicles and drivers. The three men want complete privacy to transact some business they're setting up here in America.

I'm sure that even if I understood their language I wouldn't count, I'm used to being overlooked. Even dressed as slutty as I am right now. It's ridiculous to put me into the same gear that the hostesses wear. The uniform consists of a strapless black top and black french-cut panties with a red heart sewn over the pubic mound.

Mandy and Marcie's boobs strain to escape their tube tops while I can barely keep mine up. I don't fill out the panties very well either. Neither do I have an interesting navel piercing nor a tramp stamp tattoo. I don't even have a suntan.

I do have a nice ass if you like such tight little buns that can be held in one hand but that's hardly the fashion these days. At least when I wobble about in these skyscraper high-heels there's nothing jiggling. Sad to say that's not because I'm taut and toned but because I have nothing to jiggle.

Damn, now I'm sounding whiny and miserable again. It's another symptom of being pre-heat.

After a flurry of conversation Milán leaves. He's on his way to join the party in Vista Valley, the next town over. I'm sure it will be in full swing by time he arrives. I hope he eats a bad hotdog and burps for the rest of the night making everyone pull away from his bad breath.

So now I'm here alone with my three VIPs who seem quite content to ignore me and be ignored right back. Milán told me what booze to fetch and it takes me a couple of trips to bring it all out. Scotch whiskey, American bourbon, Portuguese brandy, tumblers and snifters.

Once the drinks are taken care of I hover uncertainly not knowing what I should be doing but #3 slaps me on the butt and makes a shooing gesture. I want to give him a dirty look but after glancing into his dark shark eyes, such a dramatic contrast with is light-brown hair, I'm glad to escape while I can. Even as my body gives a little shudder of pleasurable fear. Why is it always the most handsome one who is the meanest prick? Is there a connection between beauty and a nasty nature? Maybe. That would certainly explain why Mandy and Marcie behave the way they do.

Anyhow, I scuttle away since my plan is to hide out in the kitchen, in my little nook, and try to get some sleep. I'm sure the men will make sufficient noise to wake me if they want anything – don't men always?

2

So much for grabbing a nap. We've got law enforcement driving heavy vehicles up and down the street broadcasting that everyone has to stay indoors. We're in lockdown. There's a manhunt on in the area for an escaped killer convict.

"Remain inside for your safety. Do not open windows or doors. Do not leave the premises. There's an armed and dangerous man outside. Armed police and tactical units are patrolling."

No one can enter or leave any of the properties. Anyone already on the street is being detained and questioned. Anyone breaking the rules could be shot! What if this crazed killer has already breached some place and is holding somebody hostage?

Now they're banging on the doors yelling at us to stay inside. Of course my Alpha-holes don't understand a word of it and haven't got a clue what's going on. They don't like the official-sounding announcement or the yelling. Naturally they want to go outside to see what's happening and I'm standing in front of the door shaking my head and saying *No! No! No!* Like they're going to pay the slightest bit of attention to me.

Just as they're getting ready to get rough – experience has taught me to sense when the blows are coming – we all hear a loud rapid knocking coming from the kitchen door. A muffled voice is calling so the four of us head that way. I hate to let the Alpha-holes anywhere near my hidey-hole but it can't be helped.

The rat-a-tat is loud and frenzied and the voice is becoming clearer. It's Kartal, the Beta, and he's calling out:

"Miss Lake! Miss Lake! Get my Alpha, Miss Lake! It's urgent!"

"Kartal? They're all here, I don't know which one is yours."

He doesn't bother to answer me and instead launches into their language and soon all of them are yelling at each other and back-and-forth through the door. Then Kartal switches to English explaining, to a cop I guess, what he's doing.

"Miss Lake he's taking me away! Make sure they stay inside. They MUST stay inside! I told them animals are being shot so no shifting to escape."

After a brief scuffling noise, probably Kartal being dragged up the steps to the alley, we don't hear anything more from outside. A couple of vehicle doors slam – maybe that's the police taking Kartal away?

The Alpha-holes are furious and I don't need to speak Hungarian to figure that out. There's only a small window in the kitchen which looks out onto the cement staircase since we're in the basement. The three men hurry back to look out the windows in the main room but at the A-list Gentlemens Club they're all shuttered on the outside.

Great, now we're all stuck here, and what if it's for longer than just one night? The men turn on one of the big screen TVs but nothing happens except an error message saying no signal.

I stay in the kitchen and switch on the little portable radio but there's no news broadcast. Every station is playing music because it is Saturday night, after all. I start hunting for something with a strong odor to mask my sweetening scent. I can't find any garlic but the organics bin holds the peelings from an onion. I rub it over my hands and the red heart crotch of my uniform panties and mentally cross my fingers.

I can hear the Alpha-holes from here as they bitch and complain. At least that's what I'm assuming, it all sounds very angry and destructive.

I guess I need to go see if they want anything but that's going to be tricky when I can't understand a word they say.

The irony of this lockdown is that I know all three of these Alpha-holes are murderers themselves. Probably even more dangerous than the escapee. I'm trapped inside with killers, and I'm absolutely certain these guys are armed.

3

"What do you think is going on?"

"A manhunt? That seems like an awfully convenient excuse to trap us inside."

"I don't trust coincidences and this situation stinks of a set-up."

"Do you think this is something the Fehers could have instigated?"

"I doubt it, the problems we've been experiencing at home are more of the vandalism variety. Small disturbances and annoyances rather than overt criminality. This would take a lot of preparation to stage. But maybe their American branch is tougher and smarter?"

"Maybe they've allied themselves to a bigger gang here? The business we're meeting about is extremely lucrative, we shouldn't be surprised if others are also vying for a piece of the action."

"Whether they've partnered with someone else or not – is it even possible that the Fehers could know about us?"

"I don't think so... we all took extensive precautions to travel here under the radar. Even Milán wasn't told we were coming until the last minute which is why he had to scramble to organize something for us. He'd planned on closing the Club for the night because of the fair or exposition or whatever it is."

"Exactly. That's why we chose tonight. Less people around to watch and speculate. And there were supposed to be a lot less cops around but now the street is crawling with them."

"Actually... we don't know that that's the case, do we? I mean we can hear a couple of trucks rumbling up and down and the loudhailer telling us to stay put, but we can't see them so... I'm open to believing it's a set-up."

"If so, there's nothing we can do about it except be ready to shoot whoever walks through that door, whenever that might be."

"Yeah, well, we're always prepared to do that."

The three men share a chuckle and relax back in their chairs.

"This is way too elaborate for a murder plot. They could just burst in with automatic weapons or even set fire to the building and shoot anyone who comes out."

"Except that we each have our Betas and drivers outside. But I get what you're saying. This manhunt and lockdown is probably legitimate."

The men settle down to their business discussion. They aren't concerned about Lake's presence as she flits back and forth delivering ashtrays, a table lighter, and a box of contraband Cuban cigars.

Before leaving the chef hurriedly put together a few platters of delicacies like smoked salmon, smelly cold cuts, and smellier cheeses. Dark bread, thinly sliced, and assorted crackers with little dishes of toppings, which Lake now hauls out.

I guess one of them holds caviar but I wouldn't recognize it if I tripped over it, she thinks as she carries the heavy tray.

The men talked freely around Lake. Their conversation seems to be easy and friendly yet she can feel tension in the air. She gets the impression these men don't regularly partner together but instead have a shared venture for a particular project.

It takes Lake a while to set everything out and she catches a couple of sidelong glances, as if gauging her reaction, but she truly doesn't haven't a clue what they're saying.

The Alphas only eat a bit of the food before lighting up cigars. Since no one is paying any attention to Lake she tries to sneak out unobtrusively. Janos spots her and snags her arm, dragging her onto his lap. He's bored and decides to have some fun with their reluctant hostess.

He's surprised at how little she weighs but realizes she's not just petite, she's downright skinny. Anorexic? or maybe anemic?

Looking at her small breasts in the tube top he asks what's holding this up? Of course Lake doesn't understand but Antal chuckles. Janos pulls the top over her head and when she tries to cover her breasts he easily captures her wrists and pins them behind her back. Next he studies her bare torso with a critical eye while she twists in his grasp.

Although her breasts are quite small the little mounds are nicely rounded and ride high on her chest. Her nipples are the palest pink until he tugs at one of them making it darken and harden under his touch. He spends some time teasing both her nipples while she struggles even harder against him.

He turns to Sandor who isn't interested but with gestures that even Lake can interpret Janos explains the merits of her breasts which are firm beneath her soft skin. Her young flesh has a fleeting beauty of its own.

Suddenly Janos stops talking. His cock has stiffened and he's sure it isn't because he's been toying with her hard little nipples. No, his cock has realized before his brain that *kis Tó (little Lake)* is in heat. His fondling of her tits has brought it on.

The Alphas recognized their own kind but no one considered that Lake might be an Omega. Omegas are usually pampered and cherished, not thin and neglected.

But no matter how she looks they're all on high alert since the sight, smell, and sound of her sets them snarling at each other. Lake is whimpering as she squirms in Janos' arms, trying to get away, but he holds her firmly against his chest.

The Alphas are changing before her eyes. Not shifting, but aroused and lustful, predatory and domineering. Their individual scents clog her nose and throat awakening her own desire. Their eyes have narrowed and darkened, their upper lips have skinned back showing incisors, they're growling and rumbling deep in their throats. Intense, menacing, dangerous, and combative.

It's Sandor, the oldest, who calls them to order. Young pussy does excite him but he needs a bit more time to get ready for it. He's able to control his instinctive urge to battle over the female and suggests the other two calm themselves.

They subside, somewhat, in a hair-trigger truce.

"She's an Omega and she's in heat and we're all locked in here together. This didn't just happen. We're pawns in somebody's game. It definitely is a set-up. They know we're all wolves and they might even have known her heat was coming. Somebody orchestrated this, right down to the so-called manhunt.

Well, the truth about that will come to light and when it does the situation will resolve itself. It's important that we stay strong and united against our unknown enemy. It will weaken us if we fight amongst ourselves."

They all consider his words, except Lake who doesn't understand what was said but is relieved to feel a drop in the testosterone-fueled tension. In the hopes of going unnoticed she stops struggling.

"So whoever comes to open that door will expect to see a mess of blood and bodies, thinking she'll have maddened us into killing each because of the slick from her cunt," says Antal.

Janos growls at that last phrase but visibly makes an effort to get himself under control.

"We won't be able to fight the attraction but we can enjoy taking her, all of us."

"We'll tear her apart, she must be in on it, right?"

"Only if she's suicidal," comments Sandor wryly. "No Omega would ever risk her life among strange Alphas during her heat because that's exactly what it would be: a risk of fatal proportions."

"Well the people she works for obviously don't care about her. She's a nobody who deserves whatever she gets," continues Antal with a snarl.

But Janos is getting turned on feeling Lake's body heat and hearing her mewling cries. He's a tough man who doesn't feel protective of Lake's life, but he does want to prolong it. He wants to enjoy fucking this scared *kis nyuszi (little bunny)*. His Alpha nature needs to possess the Omega.

He drags her skimpy panties off so now she's fully naked. Lifting Lake against his chest Janos hooks his forearms under her knees then pulls her legs wide open. Her pink pussy is now fully exposed and he carries her from Sandor to Antal so each man can look closely while taking a deep inhale of her scent.

First Sandor, whose eyes sparkle as he slides a finger inside testing her wetness and then licks his finger with a grin.

Next Janos carries a helplessly squirming Lake over to Antal. She's securely trapped in Janos arms – which are thicker than her legs – but manages to kick out one foot as Antal reaches towards her. She surprises him and he slaps her snatch, laughing at the fight in this feisty *kis lány (little girl)*.

Janos leans over her shoulder so he can have a good look at her cunt. Her pubic hair is the same platinum as her head hair so he can easily see her engorged lips and clitoris. The color deepening before his eyes. He can't breathe without tasting her sweet smell.

"How do we work this out?" he asks, turning to Sandor for direction.

"Let her loose," the older man orders. "She'll scamper off to hide but it won't be long before her urges drive her to come crawling back. She won't fight us. The very fact that we're Alphas will draw her in and we'll all have plenty of time to give her everything she craves."

"Everything and more! When this enforced lockdown ends we can all shift and as animals take this little she-wolf to pieces," Antal's aggression is palpable.

Fortunately for Lake she doesn't understand a word he's saying.

Janos gives Lake a hard smack on her bare ass then, with reluctance, tosses the naked girl to the floor. She crouches, fearful and mistrusting, for just a moment before getting to her feet and running towards the kitchen. Janos sends a growl after her and they all laugh when they hear her give a yipping cry.

The three men then settle back, somewhat uncomfortably now that they're aroused, to drink their brandy and smoke their cigars while they wait.

Lake is huddling in her nook in the kitchen crying. Her attempts to mask her scent were useless. She's scared of the Alphas because despite her fear she knows she can't resist them. She won't be able to control the urges brought on her by her heat and yet she can feel the violence in them. They mean her harm and she's unable to protect herself.

Her body is so aware of them being close by. Even as the tears stream down her face she's touching her hard needy nub and sliding the slick she's producing all over her labia. She presses her thighs tight together but that only makes her pussy throb with need. She has sex toys she's used during heats before but they won't stave off the lust and longing – not when there are Alphas in the vicinity.

Bowing her head Lake once again thinks: Fuck. My. Life.

4

"Can you call the little she-wolf if you send an alpha wave?" asks Antal.

"I don't think so," begins Sandor, "Let me explain by telling you what I do know. First of all I claimed my mate in the traditional manner by chasing her down, that's usual with my clan, and since we both enjoyed the run it's something we've done again and again over the years."

Sitting forward Janos asks: "And you take your mate in wolf form?" He is obviously fascinated and eager to hear the older man's reply.

"Both ways, as human and wolf. My mate is considerably younger than me and the last time we ran I'm sure she slowed down on purpose."

"She was concerned for your health?" asks Janos.

"No, she wanted to be caught," states Antal.

"Maybe yes to both, but I also suspect she wanted to be disciplined for cheating in the race."

"Ah, yes, the discipline and the sexual excitement it generates! I'm sure my mate provokes me deliberately, too!"

Tilting his head Antal gives the other two a puzzled look. They explain to him the delights he'll experience when he finds and claims his fated mate, but he looks doubtful. Many don't believe in the idea of fated mates until they meet their own.

"I've never felt the urge to bond or mark my claim, and I've never knotted," admits Antal.

Janos sits back and shakes his head in wonder telling the younger man that he's jealous thinking of the awesome experience awaiting Antal at his first time knotting.

"It's the most incredible thing and each time is just as exciting, it never gets old."

"Fated mates are special and we are lucky to have them. Mine has told me when I call her with an alpha wave she not only hears it, but physically feels it as well. She describes it as a very strong gust of wind that can actually make her stumble, while emotionally she feels dominated.

I asked her if the other she-wolves in our pack are aware when I call and she said yes but not in the same way. My wave makes her long for me but the other she-wolves don't feel any kind of attraction. Some say they feel a breeze that makes the hair on their arms stand up, while others describe a vibration like the shimmer you sometimes see in the air on a very hot summer's day."

"Let's all try to call our *kis farkas (little wolf)* and see if between the three of us we can compel her to present herself. Fucking her won't be nearly as pleasurable as having my mate but the skinny *kis lány's (little girl's)* scent is in my nose and I want to have her."

Janos alternates being chatty and friendly with domineering and cruel.

"Why not? We have the time and the girl will be willing enough once her heat takes hold."

"I'm ready to join in as well. Let's see if we can– ah! No need, look who's slinking through the door."

Three heads swivel to watch the tentative approach of the small, slender wolf. Her fur is the color of ice but the aquamarine of her eyes is just as startling and beautiful as it is when she's in human form.

Obviously she's reluctant to come forward but she's driven by her heat and the Alphas bend their wills to draw her near. She drops her body down to crawl and Antal pushes the coffee table out of the way to make room for her. The she-wolf is huffing and whining as she rolls onto her back exposing her belly to submit and surrender.

One of the Alphas growls a command at her, they're able to communicate more easily in the lupine state, so the she-wolf shifts. Lake appears, spreadeagled on the floor exposing her pussy and lifting her hips to waft her scent among the men. Janos goes into rut first and freeing his cock he pounces on the girl, driving in deep and pounding hard.

The other two lean in, hungrily watching and waiting their turn, knowing it won't be long. Antal will have her next, and then Sandor will be ready to take her. Janos finishes and Lake immediately gets up on her hands and knees waggling her butt as she spreads her legs for whichever man is behind her, her eyes flaming with lust.

Antal's cock is really thick and the way he's forcing Lake's legs to bend shows the puckering hole of her anus. It's very attractive, but her bottom is so small there's no way he'll be able to penetrate without splitting her in two. Fortunately her cunt is tight enough to satisfy.

In fact, Antal seems to have difficulty pushing all the way in. Lake is writhing against the pain yet she stretches her little hands back to pull his ass closer. She can only reach as far as his hips which she tugs at, encouraging him eagerly.

Her wriggling brings her to yet another orgasm and Antal groans appreciatively as a new gush of slick get his cock balls-deep. He pounds her without mercy until he cums explosively. Then he passes her to Sandor.

After taking his turn Sandor drops back in his chair, breathing heavily, knowing it will take some time before he is ready again. He really enjoyed fucking that tight young pussy. So pink and tender outside, so hot and wet inside. He got a good cardio workout! Now he sits back to watch the younger men share the girl again.

Once Sandor finishes Janos plucks Lake up and onto his lap. He holds her knees on his thighs and teases her clit with his dick. The girl is wild to draw him inside but he just torments her while she cries and begs to be fucked. The sight of Lake's little round bottom trembling with her need is enough to get Sandor's cock stirring again. The only English words he knows are swears and she's using all of them while she pleads with Janos.

Finally he spreads her legs and she drops down on his hard dick with a cry of triumph. Her breasts are too small to bounce but those narrow hips are pistoning up and down in a frenzy of desire. Even Janos is surprised at how the girl has taken charge and just lets her fuck him her way.

"Look how the *szuka (slut)*, fucking craves it," he calls to us laughing. "She's going crazy and I love it!"

Antal plucks her off Janos' dick and quickly turns her around, plopping her right back down again to cut off her wail of protest. She's still impaled but facing outwards, reverse cowgirl, so Antal can fuck her mouth while Janos is fucking her cunt.

Of course her little mouth is too small to take all of Antal but she strives to engulf him. He yanks her hair to pull her head up and stares into her gorgeous eyes, such an uncommon shade of blue, brimming with tears, as she strives to pleasure him, despite the struggle.

Antal gently caresses her cheek and surprises himself at the tenderness of his touch but she's working so hard to please. Saliva escapes the side of her mouth and runs down her chin, the sight of which makes him groan. He pushes harder and feels his tip touch the back of her throat. She's huffing for air and he pulls back just far enough so she can inhale a deep breath before he plunges back in again.

Janos feels his orgasm build to a crescendo while watching Lake's narrow hips and tiny butt sliding up and down on his engorged, red cock. She's really working his dick and each time he sinks deeply into her hot, tight sheath he has to fight to maintain control over his erection. It feels so very good to be inside her with her frenzied gyrations exciting him even more.

Sandor watches the younger men, admiring their stamina, but then decides an old wolf can still teach the pups an interesting technique or two. Janos is holding Lake's hips and Antal is holding her head so Sandor kneels beside the threesome and zeroes in on the vulnerably exposed clitoris of the *baba farkas (baby wolf)*.

She moans when he twiddles the sensitive nub between his thumb and fingertips but shudders to a climax when he presses down hard. Her little ass is bouncing against Janos' groin as she rides out her orgasm. Sandor doesn't hesitate before leaning in close to swirl her slick on his tongue. This orgasm makes Lake clamp down with a rapid squeezing on Janos' cock with the muscles of her pussy, while she sucks her cheeks hard along the length of Antal's cock doing her best to draw him further down her throat.

When the two men simultaneously cum and fall back Lake steps up to the kneeling man, her eyes beseeching him for more. She stands before Sandor offering the scent of her raw red pussy. He slips one of her slender legs over his shoulder and gently lowers her to the ground while pulling up the other leg. She's too short to cross her ankles behind his neck but her feet reach and can press flat against his upper chest. Spread wide open like this allows Sandor to bury his mouth in her vagina, licking and nibbling the tender flesh while her hips buck under his skillful tonguing.

Some of Antal's cum is streaked across her face and she rubs it over her lips and nose, drinking in the scent of him. Again he leans in close to watch with a hungry, possessive gaze.

Janos sits back to enjoy the performance as Sandor repeatedly brings Lake to the edge until she's crying, writhing, screaming, and begging. He lets her orgasm then forces another and yet another until she's howling.

Sandor's teasing of Lake has primed his cock for another go so he gives her a leisurely fucking, propping himself up on one arm while he uses his other hand to caress from her chin to her hips and around to cup her behind. His hand caresses everywhere except her clit and soon she's trying to grind the aching bundle of nerves against him.

Despite the girl's swiveling and squirming Sandor maintains the measured pace of his strokes until he hits her g-spot and Lake's scream signals that she's orgasmed vaginally, too. It's not until she collapses, spent, that Sandor speeds up and friction from his pubic bone torments her clit into frenzied ecstasy again.

Bravo! cries Janos, and Antal adds *fucking awesome, Silver Fox!*

Sandor gasps out a satisfied breath claiming:

"It's this *csinos róka (pretty fox),* who deserves the credit."

He smiles down at the girl but Lake is looking over his shoulder at Antal.

5

I sense a hardness, a cruelty in #3 but red flags be damned because he's drop-dead gorgeous. #1 gave me a satisfying interlude but I'm ready for more and #3 draws me to him.

My body is on fire. Heat doesn't adequately describe what I'm going through. I've undergone a few before but never in the company of a man because I was warned to always protect myself during this time. So this is my first heat experience with company and not just a man but an Alpha. And fuck me here are three of them!

Instead of satiating my hunger it just seems to grow and grow the more it's fed by these virile men.

And #3 is just... OMFG sexy, scary, steamy, sinister, seductive, spicy...

My eyes have dropped from his face down to his beautiful physique and I want to see more of him. He's taken off his shirt but still has a vest on. It's very sexy but I need to see more skin. I can only see some of his tattoos which obviously continue across his back and chest.

I scurry over as quickly as I can on my knees and start climbing up his body. He's still wearing his pants but they're unzipped. I can feel the hard muscling in his thighs and spy his uncircumcised cock settled back in its nest of curly pubic hair.

I pull up his undershirt and see muscles starting at his groin and moving up on each side of his navel. Then there's a row of muscle and another row and another – is this what they mean by a six-pack? I love the feel of him, he's so hard-bodied, so manly and macho. My little hands are here, there, and everywhere, My palms circling over his warm flesh.

There's a sprinkling of hair right across the top of his chest that grows down to his nipples. Small, hard nipples that I pinch and nip. He growls but I giggle and nibble some more. Smack! I feel his hand slam down on my ass, twice, as he says *nincs harapás (no biting)*. I don't know what the words mean but the spanks sting so I pull my teeth back and only suck and lick. I can taste the salt of his sweat.

Now I'm exploring and caressing his arms and shoulders. He's so big and muscular, I can't circle his bicep even with both hands. His tattoos are mostly black ink but there is a little color: mostly red but also a small amount of blue and green. He's an absolute work of art. He looks good, tastes good, smells good, feels fucking fantastic... I press my naked body against his chest and his torso is at least twice as wide as mine. He could wrap me in his embrace and suffocate me if he didn't crush me to bits first.

His body art ends well below his neckline. From the shoulders up he has the perfect executive look but I can sense the danger of him. Finally I bring my hands up to his handsome face and look at him fully. His mouth curves up but it isn't a pretty or happy smile. He's an apex predator, a deadly Alpha wolf and he's directing his laser focus on me. I'm melting, I'm dripping, I'm drowning.

#3 doesn't seem to know what to make of me and the feeling's mutual! His expression is faintly puzzled, and his eyes narrow as though he's trying to figure something out. We shared a moment where he handled me gently but I'm strongly attracted to his rougher, tougher side.

I'm thrilled and terrified at the same time but my sense of self-preservation prevails and I slip off him and hurry away, out of the room to recuperate

The men each lay back in their chairs, sated and happy.

"At least we don't have to worry about knotting her," comments Janos. "She's so horny she'd try to take it, too!"

Sandor chuckles before adding: "I do feel sorry for the little Omega when her heat ends and she's left with a bruised body and the pain of a very well-used cunt."

"She won't forget us in a hurry, that's for sure!"

"Except... don't we want her to forget all about us?"

"You mean... permanently?"

"Nah, no need once we deal with the traitors who tried to set us up. *Kis farkas (little wolf)* has been a good little *kurva (whore)* for us. I'll give her a nice tip and you should too."

"I gave her more than my tip. I was balls to her chin down her throat!"

"She's damn lucky she didn't provoke you into more, Antal. I've known you since we were horny kids and it always went the same way with you. After fucking you'd turn mean. Our little Tó was wise to run away when she did."

Antal smirked in reply but then changed his mind to say: "Those beautiful blue-blue eyes buy her a lot of leeway with me."

"Oh yeah? I think the only thing that curbed your usual violence was the look of absolute adoration on the *kis ringyo's* (little bitch's), face. She sure is your number one fan."

Turning to Sandor Janos continues, asking: "Those eyes do make you wonder, don't they? Especially with that platinum blonde hair. We don't often see that combination in Hungary. Anyhow, how long do you think we'll have to wait for the soon-to-be-dead men?"

"If I was the guy plotting against us I'd wait a few hours for our frenzy to peak and then burn out, but I'd definitely return before dawn."

"I'm sure that Milán is involved. He's always been a slimy, fawning piece of shit."

"What about Kartal?"

"If he's not part of the plot then they've killed him. But if he is... well, we'll kill him. Either way he's already a dead man, like the others."

"He's served in my household since he was just a child, many years ago, and I don't think he'd connive against me or us. Hopefully he got away with the police. Even if they arrest him being in jail is better than being outside."

"Can't tell what it looks like outside but I figure we've got at least another hour or so. I'm not tired so if anyone wants to grab some sleep I'll keep watch."

"I'm wide awake."

"Me too. Why don't we have a game of– oh-ho, look who's come back for more?"

"I can't," groaned Sandal.

"Oh and see? She's brought her own toys to play with..."

Janos inwardly curses himself for commenting on Antal's vicious nature, hoping he hasn't aroused that beast with its jaded and spoiled appetites. Janos enjoyed the girl's firm young body, so willing and eager. He's grateful for the pleasure she gave, and doesn't want to see Antal hurt her.

It's been some time since Janos strayed from his mate but he's an Alpha so he won't apologize or feel guilty for following his primal nature. When an Omega's scent calls it's an Alpha's nature to answer.

Lake has brought in a handful of sex toys that she drops at Antal's feet with the excitement of a puppy wanting a game of fetch. He drops down on the floor to inspect the items.

First he picks up what looks like a very large tongue and laughs when he presses a switch that sends it vibrating. His finger flicks the switch again and the vibration grows much stronger. Another flick and the tip of the tongue starts swiveling as well. That makes all the men laugh.

Antal pushes Lake down on her back and she immediately spreads her legs wide. He starts playing with the tongue-shaped vibrator and soon has her squirming. He picks up a large lime-green dildo and pushes it up inside her. It isn't self-powering so he starts roughly thrusting in and out.

He stops to insert a smaller dildo in Lake's back passage which he pushes as far as he can then leaves there. He didn't use any lube so that must have hurt but she's wantonly eager so her suffering won't hit until later. Now he resumes tormenting her folds and clit with the silicone tongue while fucking her with the big toy.

Sandor and Janos are leaning forward to watch the skinny girl grimace with endurance while greedily demanding it all. Antal easily flips her onto her hands and knees, removing the big dildo and replacing it with his even larger cock. He leaves the smaller one plugging her ass and continues holding the pulsating tongue to her clit, set high for maximum action. Securing her tightly in place with his forearm across her throat she's delirious with lust and choking, squeezing her own small breasts and twisting her nipples.

Her body bucks, shakes, and writhes. Antal's cock must be hitting her G-spot simultaneously with the tongue toy giving her a clitoral orgasm. She gives the high-pitched yip-yip-yipping cry of her sex and Antal joins her with a deep-throated howl.

Hearing that sends the girl out of her mind.

As an unmated shifter Antal is enjoying her in ways the other two can't. They couldn't help but respond to the smell of the Omega's slick, but they both have fated mates who will know of their Alpha's rutting.

Sandor's mate will demand to be bedded immediately so she can erase the memory of the Omega he's fucked, while Janos will be berated by his lady until he grows frustrated enough to discipline her. Corporal punishment will drive them to hungry, violent sex until she gives in with loving submission.

Anticipating his homecoming Janos smiles to himself. He is madly in love with his wife and it does feel like madness with him craving her body just as much as he did when they first met. Now he has another reason to be grateful for the Omega's service.

Finished, Antal removes the toys and tosses them aside. He stretches out on his back on the plush carpet, showing off his perfect physique. From his long muscular legs to the indent between groin and buttocks, the curve of his back muscles lifts his powerful arms up. He pulls Lake on top of him. She's so slender and small she looks like a child lying on his chest.

"I wonder if someone is deliberately keeping her half-starved so that her body stays under-developed and adolescent?" muses Janos aloud.

Sandor considers for a moment before shaking his head saying: "No, there's been no sign of a protector and no indication anyone is taking any care of the *kis lány (little girl)*. I think she's been rejected and abandoned as the runt of the litter. There's probably no place for her to go so she stays here and gets bullied."

Antal rubs his hands over her sides, feeling from her visible ribs down to her jutting hipbones, and comments that she is badly undernourished.

"I think I'll bring her along when we leave. I'll get her properly fed and that should put some womanly curves on her. Padding here," he massages her small bottom, "and here," he adds, fondling her small breasts.

Alarmed, Janos quickly looks to Sandor but the older Alpha just shrugs. There's nothing they can do if Antal wishes to take the girl, they have no right to stop him. Sandor frowns in concern, thinking of stories he's heard about the younger Alpha, but he's not prepared to battle with him over this *csinos baba (pretty baby)*. Janos hasn't seen Antal for some time and acknowledges that he's grown into a healthy, handsome man. Lake certainly is smitten with him and maybe that will save her.

"Once her heat ends–" begins Sandor but Antal interrupts saying:

"It's more than just being in heat with this one, she's made for fucking. Once I get her healthy she'll be ready to take it hard and often. I'll share her with my Beta and maybe one or two others. She'll love it and if she doesn't well... she'll learn. I look forward to teaching her new ways to please me. I like the idea of educating her."

"She probably doesn't even have a passport."

"No, I'll keep her at my home here. I never go back to Hungary these days but if I want to well, there are people I could reach out to, people who frequently move young women from one country to the next, to solve that problem."

"Human traffickers, *baszós (fuckers)*. Why would you trade with them?"

"Sandor, we're killers. Do we really get to make distinctions?"

"Absolutely yes! There are degrees of evil and I've made my peace with what I've done. Right or wrong, I believe I made the best choices for the situations at the time. I have killed but I have never sold another human being. Ugh, I find the idea as repugnant as cannibalism!"

Antal respects the older Alpha and considers Sandor's words before replying:

"I will keep her here then. She can be the mistress of my home, making me look more respectable."

"I never thought I'd say this but I think you've finally met a *kis farkas (little wolf)* who has gotten under your skin, Antal."

"This skinny girl? She hardly has tits. I like *nagy cicik (big tits)*, round and bouncy that I can grab by the handful and squeeze hard. This girl's small pink nipples are pretty, I guess, but I'm used to seeing a really big brown circle around a dark nipple. And I want a woman with a *kövér szamár (plump ass)*. When I fuck her in the bum I want to sink between huge mounds of soft flesh. Something that wobbles if I paint it with handprints, not her little behind that I can barely pinch."

"Exactly my point! This *baba róka (baby fox)* is nothing at all like the women you normally bed and, let's be honest, abuse. With your looks you've had many, many opportunities with a huge variety of women. You always preferred voluptuous beauties with dark coloring but you never made any of them a mistress. This little one makes you feel protective."

"I don't know about that... but maybe it's true and I'm attracted because she is so different. I'm still going to pass her around to my friends."

"Only because you love watching them service your woman especially when you're joining in on the fun. Sharing her turns you on, but after tonight I have to admit that I'm sure she'll enjoy it too."

Lake couldn't react to this even if she understood the words because she'd fallen into an exhausted sleep even before Antal finished pulling the dildo from her ass.

6

Now that Antal has laid some sort of claim on Lake neither Janos nor Sandor have another go with the girl. Instead they enjoy the show Antal puts on for them. He's happy to have her all to himself, feeling a bit possessive after all.

His fingers keep straying to her anus, circling the puckered rim. He knows he's far too big for her but is obviously thinking about how he can train this muscle and stretch her out. He'll get her accustomed to wearing butt plugs in gradually bigger sizes, and then shallowly penetrating with one finger and then more.

Anal sex is a favorite of his that's been enjoyed by many of his partners, too. He knows women can experience deep pleasure from gentle pressure applied to their PS-spot, particularly when his fingers are strumming their clit at the same time. The *kis baba (little baby)* doesn't flinch when he explores her back passage so he knows he can look forward to introducing her to this type of intercourse.

When he first arrived at the Club he only gave her the barest of glances but Lake's heat has turned her into an eager and exciting sexual partner, and awakened appetites he will exploit. Nibbling her neck makes her shiver and when he wraps his hand around her throat he can feel her whole body tremble with greedy lust and longing and fear.

Antal senses she's drawn to his darkness, despite seeing the wariness in her eyes. He already knows he'll enjoy pampering her tenderly after he's hurt her in their playtime. It's a new way of thinking and feeling for him.

Lake's cunt is drowning in her slick and the three Alpha's cum. It's been stretched, pounded, and rubbed raw till it's swollen and red yet still a pulse beats that craves being filled with cock. She twists her body until she's positioned over Antal's dick and gives little mewling cries. He reaches down to wet his fingers and inhaling the scent deeply groans as the need to rut grabs hold of him.

His wolf is desperate to come out so he growls at Lake as warning then starts to shift. She quickly changes too to accommodate this Alpha who is already mounting the pale-furred she-wolf. Her cries of utter submission drive the much bigger beast to worry her neck ruff with his sharp teeth and even nip her shoulders. She drops down, splaying her forelegs and raising her hind and tail to better serve her master.

Soft growls escape both Sandor and Janos as they witness the animal coupling. It's a sight more commonly seen when they've shifted themselves and are with their pack.

They're aroused by Lake's scent, her slick, her pheromones, her yipping cries, and her complete surrender but they know it's too dangerous to attempt to join in. Antal will not be willing to share in this form. The air is heavy with the feral odor of mating wolves, and with wild grunts and growls and howls.

When Antal returns to his human form he has to shake his *kis farkas (little wolf)* awake. He's not sure if Lake is sleeping or passed out. She's certainly worn out. He bites her ear to rouse her into shifting. Then she curls her naked girl's body in his lap and immediately falls asleep again.

"I think I'd better get dressed," he announces, sliding Lake onto the chair while he stands to hunt for his clothes. "It must be almost time for our enemy to arrive."

The three Alphas give each other wary looks. At some point in the night it's occurred to each of them that the enemy might already be inside and just waiting for his cohorts to breech the doors. They've all worked together for many years but each runs his own business privately.

They hear the outside door open and approaching footsteps.

The men ready their guns and stand in easy firing positions, apart from each other.

"Ooooh I smell sex!" exclaims Mandy in a loud, laughing voice that wakes up Lake.

"Sorry, did I burp? Marcie giggles and the women chuckle at the old joke.

"Shut up, you two!" snarls Milán. "I can't hear anything."

"Well, you won't, will you? They must all be dead by now so move, I want to see!"

"But we should be able to smell blood and shit and–"

Milán comes to an abrupt halt when he enters the room with the two hostesses bumping into him from behind. All three stand in open-mouthed shock to be facing the Alphas with their weapons cocked.

"Tell us who is behind this Milán and your death will be quick otherwise..." The chill in Sandor's voice has Milán stuttering to deny and excuse and explain when the loud bang of a gunshot sounds and Marcie crumples to the ground.

Mandy lets out a high-pitched shriek and Lake feels a measure of satisfaction that it's finally her nemesis' turn to be frightened and trembling. A second shot cuts off the scream and Mandy joins her best friend in death.

Damn, that happened too quick, thinks Lake.

Milán is gabbling and gasping, unable to utter a word. Antal strides forward, kicking aside a long tanned leg, to grab Milán by the throat. Milán's head flops back and forth as Antal shakes him. Lake recognizes the vicious threat in his tone and body language, even though she can't understand the Hungarian words.

Eventually Milán finds his voice and begins speaking rapidly, desperately, while the three Alphas fire questions at him and, apparently, more threats.

Antal tosses Milán aside and the other three confer, arguing a little before reaching a decision. Janos delivers a hard punch to Milán's throat and there's no emotion on their faces as they watch the man choke and strangle for air. Milán collapses in spasms.

Lake absorbs the horror of sudden violent death with equanimity. Those three had tormented her for so long that she can only be glad they will no longer hurt her. She looks at the Alphas resigned to the fact that as a witness she'll now become their next victim.

They don't even spare her a glance as they continue their conversation. *What Alpha-holes,* Lake thinks. Then her breathing speeds up as she realizes what's in store. Now she *wants* to be ignored and unnoticed.

"So we were right about the Fehers being a threat."

"Those Jew bastards–"

"Yeah, yeah we can be angry later. Right now we need to fix things up here."

"We need to check the situation outside."

"Everything should be okay since the whole manhunt was just a ruse."

"Yeah, but we heard Kartal and a cop, more than one cop because of the loudspeaker–"

"I've been thinking about that and I think we would have been the only ones to hear it because this is a quiet area with nothing open at night. That's why the Club is situated here."

"But Kartal translated the broadcast for us."

Sandor sighs deeply saying: "Then he was in on it."

"Maybe not," comments Janos. "Maybe he was fooled as well before being dragged away by that cop, or pretend cop."

"We need to see what's going on outside."

The three exchange looks then their eyes slide over to Lake scrunched down in the chair. She's trying to make her small self look even smaller, negligible, unimportant. Antal picks up the undershirt he'd left off when he dressed in a hurry and motioning Lake to stand he puts it on her. It hangs like a dress, a very low-cut cheap-looking dress.

He leads her down the passage to the door. Lake gazes up at him with her lovely aquamarine eyes huge in her face. Antal gives her a kiss – the first kiss she's had from any of the men – and slips behind the door gun at the ready before opening it.

Lake steps outside feeling the chilly dawn air send shivers down her bare arms and legs. Stepping towards the street, empty of vehicles except for Milán's luxury sedan, her bare feet quickly grow cold on the pavement. She looks left and right but sees nothing and no one.

Lake is just starting to question the whole manhunt and lockdown idea. Where were the police? How did Milán, Mandy, and Marcie get into the Club if the police hadn't unblocked the doors? And why would they do that and then just walk away?

Unless Milán told them the Club is empty, she thinks. But there still should be some sign of something having happened...

Antal steps out behind her, pointing his gun, and just then a relieved shout of happiness echoes in the deserted road. Kartal appears around a corner, arms wide and grinning. Antal almost shoots him but, thankfully, holds back and is instead embraced by Sandor's Beta.

Antal is relieved to see his own Beta, Grigor, following behind. Antal signals to him explaining that he needs Grigor to head straight back to their compound. He's very concerned about an attack, possibly arson, and wants to be sure the property is under guard.

Grigor says he'll hire a car but Antal tells him to take their limo, there's no time to waste, and he'll make other arrangements. Grigor complies and leaves immediately.

Kartal has been waiting impatiently and now speaks all in a rush saying:

"I thought you were all dead! Is my Alpha okay? What's been going on? I saw those three go in just now and I've been standing here wondering what I should do. That fake policeman dumped me far away but I managed to get back eventually and I've been hiding and waiting..."

They can hear the strain in his voice as it trails off and then Sandor and Janos are coming through the door so Kartal rushes to his Alpha.

Antal notices the shivering girl in his undershirt and beckons her, calling Tó.

Lake stares back at him, uncertainty and fear written all over her face, but she points to herself and replies: "Lake. My name is Lake."

Antal now gestures impatiently saying: "Lake, Tó," he shrugs dramatically before continuing in halting English: "You is Tó. My *kis lány, kis farkas (little girl, little wolf)*. My Tó."

Well okay, I guess I'm Tó now, she thinks, *but at least it's better than being called Puddle.*

When everyone is back inside they sit down to discuss the situation. Tó's sleep has refreshed her body and her libido. Despite Antal touching a finger to her lips meaning shush she sits on his lap making whiny little cooing sounds and squirming. Exasperated he sets her on her feet and holds her hand over her vagina, giving a few strokes to mime masturbation, and with a swat on her ass waves her off to the kitchen.

Janos laughs at the frustrated Alpha saying: "I knew it, I told you so!"

While Sandor just shakes his head adding: "Better you then me, Antal. I'm too old to keep up with the needs of that little nympho."

Kartal looks from one man to the other and his Alpha explains: "Tó went into heat and we've all enjoyed pleasuring ourselves with her but she's insatiable. I know you'd never to think it to look at her but that little *farkas baba (wolf baby)* is dynamite."

"You can have her too if you want, Kartal," says Antal, "but first you need to tell us your side of things because we're still in the dark about what went on last night."

"I'll tell you what I can but... don't you want me to get rid of these bodies first?"

"No, we'll probably leave them here, just as is. We haven't gotten that far yet in our plans. Tell us what you know and then we'll make some decisions."

"Can we get Tó to make us coffee?" asks Janos but Antal shakes his head saying:

"God, no! She'll probably put Viagra in it."

"Let me get the coffee, it won't take long, and we can sit comfortably," says Kartal jumping up and heading to the kitchen.

Sandor sighs saying: "He likes to serve and he'll just keep fussing until he can so we might as well just let him do this. Then we'll keep him talking until he's told us everything twice over."

"Do you think your girl will proposition him in the kitchen?" Janos asks Antal.

"I'm sure she will, but he'll turn her down. Maybe after we've had our talk I can persuade him to take her while we watch. I want to get her used to performing for me."

"Yeah, you're hooked, you're keeping her. I just wondered, though... have you seen her eyes?"

"Of course I have—"

"No, I mean that color."

"I know what you mean but no, it can't be all that rare because obviously she's come out of a gutter, so in America it's probably not so unusual."

"Hey! Kartal must really be wondering now. I mean, he knows we thought we were in a police lockdown yet he arrives to find dead bodies, a stink of sex, and a naked Omega oozing slick yet the three Alphas are sitting around amicably. That's got to be confusing the hell out of him!"

True to his word Kartal returned shortly after carrying a tray with two carafes, cups, and fixings. He'd also scrounged around and found some cold cuts and bread rolls.

He begins by apologizing for everything that has happened and the discomfort his Alpha has gone through. He adds that he's also sorry for slapping the Omega but she wouldn't stop pestering him in the kitchen. The men laugh and that breaks the tension.

While serving a hot coffee to each of the Alphas he begins his story about the previous night, telling them that he'd been talking and sharing a smoke with the other Alpha's drivers when things kicked off.

Sandor interrupts to ask where the drivers are now and Kartal explains they scattered at what they all thought were police but he has their cellphone numbers and is in touch so they'll be available as soon as the Alphas are ready to leave.

Shortly after the Club staff left a policeman appeared walking towards the Alphas' employees at the same time that a van with a loudspeaker slowly drove along the street announcing the lockdown and manhunt. The drivers got in their cars and left but Kartal stayed to find out what was going on. The policeman wouldn't allow that and shooed him away from the Club's front door.

That's when Kartal ran around to the back where the kitchen was but the policeman followed and dragged him away back up the stairs from the basement. The van was waiting and its driver helped the policeman put Kartal in the back. He fought them but they had a taser.

When Kartal came to he was in an unfamiliar and deserted-looking place but since he still had his phone he was able to get back to the Club using his GPS. The sky was just beginning to lighten when he arrived. There was nobody on the street or in any of the surrounding buildings. He didn't even know if his Alphas were still at the Club.

"Why didn't I think to phone you?" exclaimed Sandor. "Why didn't you phone me?"

"There's no signal here. It's been jammed or something. When I call a recorded voice just comes on telling me service is not available."

"Remember? We thought they'd shut off news on the TV, a media blackout, but maybe it was just somebody jamming the signal?"

"Well whatever it is it's still jammed, but only in this Club. My phone works fine out on the sidewalk. I can call anyone, I just couldn't call you."

"Okay, so keeping us incommunicado was part of the plot. Yes, I see that. Go on."

"There's not a lot more to tell. I didn't have to wait too long before Milán showed up with the two waitresses and I heard, very faintly, what sounded like two gunshots. Then Lake came outside half-naked and Antal followed her."

The Alphas considered his words silently for a minute or so. Then Janos confirmed to Kartal that he had heard gunfire when Sandor shot the two women. He also passed on what they'd learned from Milán before Janos himself killed him with a single blow.

"It was the Feher gang behind all this. They had to put it all together quickly because we didn't give much notice about our meeting here so maybe that made them sloppy. Worked out good for us."

"They tried to use our dual natures against us, this server they left us with went into heat. We could have killed each other over her. They look down on us for being wolves."

"Well, we look down on them for being Jews."

"We didn't win a battle here, we simply outmaneuvered and eluded their trap. Now we need to bring the fight to them."

"Now you're talking!" Antal said, his eyes bright with battle lust. Janos nods and leans forward to join in the planning.

"I propose we just walk away from this. Maybe the police will think it's a robbery. Our fingerprints will be few among the many, Janos your gun is untraceable, right? and we'll go our separate ways for now. Antal, I know you'll be staying on here, well in a different city, so you can keep us posted on developments in this matter, plus get started on the venture that brought us here in the first place."

"You and I can reach out to our sources back home to get a lead on how best to hit back at the Fehers," said Janos. "We'll bring those *baszós (fuckers)* down."

The four men nod their agreement just as Tó comes into the room shyly but with determination. Antal's vest looks ridiculous on her. Walking over he pulls the undershirt over her head so she's naked again, then lifts her up and onto Kartal's lap. The Beta is startled to be straddled by the naked Omega who doesn't hesitate to show him what she wants.

"You've been through quite an ordeal tonight and this morning, Kartal. Now it's your turn to relax and enjoy our *kis nyuszi (little bunny)*. We want to see her work her magic on you."

"Well, Alpha... if it's okay with you... and with Lake–"

She interrupts to tell him "Antal says I am Tó now."

Sandor smiles his permission to the young man who doesn't need a moment's more encouragement before turning his attention to the girl who has wrapped her arms around his neck.

Running his hands down her back to her hips, over her bottom, along her thighs, until his fingers find her vagina and penetrate while thumbing her clit. Tó responds by reaching for his pants to free his cock. Her hunger makes her greedy and she squeals with pleasure over Kartal's hard dick.

No further foreplay is required, both of the young people are ready and they happily begin fucking, Tó bouncing up and down on Kartal's thighs while he holds her hips to lift her high up on his cock before slamming her down again. They orgasm together and while he lies back panting Tó slides down to her knees between his legs and licks him clean. Of course that's enough to make a man his age hard enough for another go.

Kartal joins Tó on the floor and grabbing hold of her ankles lifts her legs up and back, pinning them at her shoulders. Now she is stretched wide open and the Alphas are treated to the sight of her very red and swollen labia and her shiny wet clitoris. They are highly entertained watching Kartal rub his hard dick along her slit, making Tó writhe and beg with desire.

The two youngsters speak English but the Alphas don't need any knowledge of that language to understand that Tó is begging and pleading to be fucked. Janos studies Antal as he intently watches the couple on the floor climax again. Sensing eyes on him he looks up and catches Janos' stare. Janos winks, saying:

"Antal, when you and Tó leave you might have to drive the car and let your driver have a go, too."

Antal simply growls. Now that the young people have finished he stands and drags Tó to her feet telling Kartal to instruct her to pack up her things because they're going now. After the words are spoken he follows her to her nook in the kitchen to fetch her stuff. There isn't much and she gathers it up quickly.

"I sent Grigor home in my car so I need to hire another, can Kartal take care of that for me?"

"He can, his English is very good, but take the car and driver I hired. After this little incident Sandor and I are anxious to get back home as quickly as possible so we can ride together to the airfield. It's not like we need to keep our heads down anymore."

7

Less than an hour has passed since I fully expected to be shot dead. I figured after Mandy and Marcie I'd be next. I've had a pretty shitty life so it's like totally unfair to have it end so soon and so badly. My mind just kind of froze on that thought and I didn't imagine anything further, but here I am in a fancy limo, well I guess there isn't any other kind, going somewhere with Antal. The best-looking, but also the meanest, of the Alphas.

After I changed into leggings and a hoodie I stuffed my pathetically small amount of personal possessions into a grocery bag and walked out of the Club forever. Antal led me to the back door of the car and put me inside. It smells rich just like the lounge of the Gentlemens Club, well like it smelled before the gunshots and blood.

The seat is soft leather and I sink right down into it. It feels about ten times better than my bed! The windows are tinted and there's also tinted glass separating the back from the front. It's totally private back here. Private and very roomy. And I'll be all alone with Antal.

Maybe he's planning to kill me somewhere else? But since they've already got three bodies littering the Club it really doesn't make sense to dispose of me elsewhere. Unless they're trying to throw suspicion on me? If it appears that I've run away I'll look guilty for those murders.

Counting the driver there's two of them and they're both huge so I guess I'm going on an adventure, huh! I don't have anywhere else to go, and I certainly don't want to stay here and have to explain to the police why I'm the only one still alive.

It's not like I've got the greatest of relationships with the cops as it is.

Since I'm already in the car I guess the decision was made without my input which is kinda the story of my life. I wonder where we're going? I suppose it really doesn't matter and if it's truly awful well, I'll just run away and fend for myself. It won't be the first time I've had to do that.

So I leave Lake behind and follow my alpha-hole as he leads the way.

I really am Tó now.

8

It's been a long drive to get here, we even stayed overnight at a hotel *en route* but I slept through that experience. I've been so comfortable lying back on the upscale upholstery of this sleek sedan. I started off on Antal's lap and we kissed again which was weird but nice. Hot and passionate but somehow tender, too. I like kissing him but my pussy's need is greater.

I slip off him onto my back and stripping off my two piece outfit - I didn't bother putting on a thong - lie splayed out and open for him. His eyes travel up and down my nude body before he teases a nipple and then strokes my clit. He slip one, two, then three fingers inside me while his thumb keeps circling my super-sensitive nub. He crooks his fingers inside me to find my g-spot and that's a new experience that has me going off like a firecracker.

Since there are only the two of us in the back of this very roomy car it's easy enough for him to fuck me in several positions which we both enjoy. He always brings me to orgasm and I don't know if that's planned or a happy bonus. I'm not convinced he cares about my pleasure but... he does like watching me fall apart and seems to take a certain pride in himself when I do.

Eventually he's had enough even though I'm still itching for more. When I try to stroke and kiss his cock he pushes me away with a growl. I can't understand what he says but I definitely hear the name Janos while he shakes his head. I guess he's recalling something that #2 said about me.

Anyhow, he raps a coded knock on the smoked glass divider that separates us from the driver. The car slows then pulls over to the side of the road before stopping. Both Antal and the driver get out and have an exchange in their own language for a minute or two. Then Antal ducks back in long enough to position me over the seats and pinch my bottom while wagging his finger in my face. It feels like I'm being warned to behave or obey or something.

He leaves and the door opens to admit the driver. Poor man, he's greeted by the sight of me naked and spread, ready to fuck. Antal has placed my forearms on the opposite seat with my knees on the edge and my legs wide apart, fully exposing my pussy. All the driver has to do is kneel down between the two rows of seats in order to plug into me.

The car starts to move and I realize Antal is now doing the driving! Startled I lift my head up and he's lowered the privacy glass so I see him clearly. And he watches me, too.

I have no idea what my partner's name is. Turning my head around to look at him I see that he's a big, older man whose face shows he's spent a lot of time in a boxing ring. Our eyes meet and his expression is almost apologetic. Despite being a real bruiser of a guy he handles me gently.

Stroking his cock he stares into my face before shifting his gaze to my wet and welcoming cunt. I hear him inhale deeply as he lean in to catch the scent of my slick. He likes it even though it doesn't drive him to rut since he's not an Alpha. His approval rumbles deep in his chest, a sound that only adds to my arousal, so I wiggle my hips and bum at him. He lunges forward and with one thrust pushes himself in me. I spasms around the thickness of him and draw him in all the way.

He pumps a few times before sitting back in the other seat and pulling me with him. Rocking back and forth he fucks me long and slow. Soon I'm squirming towards an orgasm while he only slightly quickens his pace. I beg for rougher manhandling but my pleading only makes him give a deep, contented sigh. My pussy is working overtime squeezing and pulsing around his dick but he maintains control until I'm a helpless wreck shattering around him.

I catch Antal staring at me through the rear-view mirror. The heat of his gaze is so intense it burns right through me. I lick my lips and realize just how much I like performing for my devilishly handsome Alpha. Even while watching another man fuck me we both know I belong to Antal. He slowly, wickedly, smiles and it thrills me that I am his.

Meanwhile the driver keeps going. Slow, steady strokes that bring me to the precipice again and again my swiveling hips dancing on his cock until I explode once more. What endurance he has! Although now I can feel him growing harder and moving faster. That encourages me to move harder and faster with him and – at last! – his breathing quickens and blows heavily against the back of my neck. I hear a groan that seems to build from his belly to surface in a roar as he shoots an endless hot stream of cum inside me, shaking me into a third orgasm.

Finally I felt fulfilled and sated. He clasps me in a bear hug before carefully pulling my legs up and over until I've been turned, with his semi-hard dick still inside me, and we are face-to-face.

No, he isn't a handsome man but his eyes are kind and his cock is amazing. With a light touch he brushes the hair back from my brow and runs his finger over my lips. Looking down he studies my small tits before running the palm of one hand over both my nipples. They grow hard again and wonder of wonders so does he!

My arms barely reach around his thick neck but I manage to hold on to him while he grasps my hips to slide me up and down, all the while looking into my eyes. I use my thighs to help push and soon I'm rapidly working his shaft. I think of Antal watching in the rearview mirror and that makes me shimmy faster.

With one big hand flat on my back to hold me he arcs me back so he's able to see my pussy moving on his dick and leaving a shiny, wet trail. He watches greedily and I grin back at him.

Now I bring my feet up, bracing myself on the seat, while I stretch and strain in a frenzy. With only the merest touch on my clit he sends me gyrating helplessly, wrapped up in the swoon of orgasmic pleasure. Still he keeps moving me up and down and up and down. I'm delirious in my half-consciousness yet I feel the insides of my passage still grabbing and clutching onto him. When I start rocking my hips in a counterpoint rhythm he responds with deep-felt passion.

Now our genitals are battling against each other and the erotic sensations are drowning me in waves of pleasure. It feels like it's too much but I want to hold on as long as I can to make this wonderful sensation last longer.

He cums with a shout while pulling me tight against him and I breathe in his lightly sweaty smell while murmuring kisses along his throat. A couple of tremors and he's completely emptied himself in me.

I love it. I felt the same way with Kartal. It's like I can fuck these non-Alphas as an equal, they don't have the power to crush me like the others did. With these men I'm a woman, not just an Omega she-wolf being taken by a rutting dominant.

The car began slowing and my partner quickly wipes himself with a handkerchief and straightens his clothes. He is ready to jump out the moment the vehicle stops but pauses for me when I reach up to kiss his cheek. He has a lovely smile.

Switching places Antal chats a bit with the driver before climbing back inside. I later learn that he is confirming the driver's suspicions that we are being followed.

Antal takes one look at my flushed face and dreamy eyes and chuckles. Lifting me onto his lap he pushes my head against his chest and wraps me loosely in his arms. I feel him place light kisses on my forehead and whisper *mine* moments before I fall asleep. I barely awoke when we arrived and Antal carried me, still naked, into my new home.

Apparently I slept for two days solid. My heat has ended.

Part Two

Once I got my strength back I realized this was a shorter heat than usual. I think that might be due to quantity and quality: tons of sex and with Alphas.

The Alpha I'm living with now still wants to fuck constantly, even though I'm no longer sending out slick-scented pheromones. He seems to really enjoy my skinny little body, and I just want to touch him all the time. I don't need to be in heat to cream my panties just by looking at his gorgeous face and listening to his sensual rumbling voice.

Except I never get to wear panties.

Small price to pay for living in this freaking mansion. It's all marble floors and wood-paneled walls, velvet drapes pooling on Persian carpets, huge flat-screen TVs in every room... every comfort and I'm luxuriating in it.

And the food! I have never, ever in my whole miserable life had enough to eat. Every meal I ate left me craving more and I was always hungry. Always. But not anymore.

I eat until my stomach hurts. Antal thinks it's hilarious. I burped the other day and he laughed so hard there were tears in his eyes. God knows if he'll survive me farting!

I'm smiling as I think this because I just feel so good. I get plenty of sleep, lots to eat, I'm warm and comfy and there's an oh-so handsome man wanting to wrap his arms around me every chance he gets. If I'm dreaming I truly never want to wake up.

So I have to say that life here, with Antal, is wonderful except... yeah, of course there's always a catch, right? Antal is great about 25 per cent of the time. And when I say great I mean he's funny and loving and kind. The exact opposite of what he's like the remaining 75 per cent. Then he's stern, cold, and cruel.

On the plus side we've discovered that we share a few kinks. Actually, Antal just does whatever he wants with me and luckily I enjoy most of it. And I've learned to keep quiet about the things I don't like so much because, well... he's got a mean streak and he'll torment me even more.

Happily ever after never really does happen in real life, does it? There's a saying I can't remember about roses and thorns, but compared to the Gentlemens Club – which at that point was the highlight of my life – I choose this bed of roses.

The only awkward bit is filling my time. I'm used to working long hours at non-stop drudgery so I don't miss not having a job but I need to find something to do. I don't really have a role here, I'm certainly not the lady of the manor. I'm not even the housekeeper. There already is a woman doing that job and I stay out of her way. She's very efficient and she's Hungarian, as are all the staff, and if they speak English they sure don't do it around me.

Antal doesn't go out to work but he spends a lot of time in his office on the phone or on his computer. He's got a keyboard in his own alphabet. He also does video conferences and likes to have me kneeling between his legs when he's online. The fact that he can't interrupt or pause the live call gives me free rein to be as naughty as possible.

Well, I'm not just going to quietly suck his dick when I can be vibrating it by humming and tickling his balls and trying to poke a finger up his ass. Every now and then I'll hit a particularly sensitive spot and his leg will involuntarily jerk, or he'll gasp, and then I have to hold in my giggles. While still keeping his cock firmly in my mouth.

Sometimes he even enjoys my antics but usually he punishes me by driving deep down my throat until I'm pleading with my teary eyes, desperate to catch a breath. He'll spurt hot and fast then slowly pull back ordering me to leave whatever I haven't swallowed in my mouth coating my tongue. He communicates this to me by squeezing my face with his strong fingers. After spending some time eyeballing me he'll gesture to open up so he can see his cum before he allows me to swallow it down. If I fail to understand he doesn't hesitate to slap me.

At other times he'll abuse me with no provocation. On those occasions I've learned to hold back my tears for as long as I possibly can. I'm unable to stifle every moan or twitch but if I can take whatever he gives me without complaint he'll be extremely loving and tender afterwards. I'm amazed to discover that he really enjoys cuddling me. His mood swings are epic.

He's learned to say good girl and that's a phrase I love to hear.

But indulging in sex play can only take up so many hours of the day. I need more.

I can't leave the property but there is quite an extensive kitchen garden so I've taken to hanging around out there. The old gardener seems quite nice and he's identified some weeds for me so I can pull them up and help out.

The walled garden is a sun-trap and it's nice being out in the fresh air. I've discovered I enjoy grubbing around in the dirt figuring maybe my inner wolf likes getting back to nature.

At break time the gardener, whose name I can't pronounce, goes into the kitchen for a bowl of sugar and when he comes back we peel rhubarb and eat it sugar-dipped. I never had rhubarb before but it sure tastes good.

The next day Antal comes out and joins us for a snack. The old man loves having the boss here, he sweeps his arms around the garden and talks so fast he can barely draw breath. Antal gives the impression he's listening intently but his eyes keep straying towards me.

I have no idea what any of this means.

2

Antal is hollering his rage throughout the house. He's yelled so much his voice is hoarse, and Tó is wisely staying out of his way. She has no idea what's wrong, but it started with a phone call that drove Antal to his computer and whatever he brought up on the screen made him furious.

She's been slinking around corners trying to keep tabs on Antal's whereabouts while keeping hers hidden. If he wasn't so angry he'd be able to sense when she was near, but if that was the case she wouldn't have to avoid him. Besides, once he bellows *Tó? Tó? Tó?* she'd better be close enough to show up pronto.

Now he and Grigor are yelling even though it sounds like they're in agreement. Such noisy drama... Tó wonders if she'll ever know what it's all about. The life she led on the streets taught her a valuable lesson about keeping her curiosity in check. As a result she's very good at closing her eyes, ears, and mind to other people's business. Just as well now that she's living in the house of a crime boss. So she won't ask and Antal isn't likely to volunteer the information.

This trouble, whatever it is, has nothing to do with her so she figures it's a good idea to hide out in the garden. At least she can enjoy the warm weather and maybe the gardener will give her something to eat.

Tó is happily uprooting vegetables and filling baskets with the food when Antal appears, blocking out the sun. Looking up she can't see his face, just his silhouette, but there's something ominous in his stance. He exhales a gusty breath that makes her assess herself from his viewpoint. She's got dirt up to her forearms, all over her knees, and probably a streak or two on her face. Looking at her hands she sees that her fingernails are rimmed in black.

When Antal takes a step back she correctly interprets this as her cue to get up and go with him into the house. He follows close behind and she can hear his loud breathing – not a good sign.

She'd like to go clean up but once indoors she hesitates, not sure what he's got in mind. Seems he agrees that she needs to wash as he propels her up the stairs to his big bathroom with the oversized shower. While Tó is undressing Antal turns on the water but only the cold tap. Tó looks at him sideways but he simply raises an eyebrow. With a pouty sigh she steps under the icy stream and her skin is immediately covered in goosebumps.

Quickly scrubbing the dirt off she slides in front of the taps and sneaking one hand behind her back she twists on the hot water. Tó loudly moans while using her other hand to soap between her legs and for a minute or so Antal is distracted by her performance. He reaches out to tweak a hard nipple and discovers the water has warmed up. Next thing Tó knows she's back against the tile wall with Antal's hand tight around her throat while he spins the hot water tap off. Now they're both standing under the cold spray.

He's fully dressed and kept warm by his anger but she shivers as her lips turn blue. She's not strong enough to fight her way out of this predicament so she relies on her weakness instead. She lets her eyes roll back and her body slump, legs collapsing as she falls to the floor only held up by the hand wrapped around her throat. Tó pretends to faint and Antal is forced to scoop her up in his arms. His growl tells her he's suspicious so she's very careful to remain limp and passive.

Grumbling under his breath in a threatening way Antal carries her into the bedroom and lays her down. He strips out of his wet shirt and pants then covers her cold wet body with his own naked flesh. Tó expels a puff of air and slowly opens her eyes. Antal has always found her aquamarine eyes mesmerizing and this time is no different. They spend a long moment simply gazing at each other.

"Kiss?" she suggests but he barely glances at her mouth before shaking his head.

"Tó sickness?"

"No, I just couldn't breathe, I couldn't get air."

She fans her fingers as if brushing air into her mouth. He tilts her head back and studies her throat. Tracing his fingers across the sides of her neck she suspects he's bruised her and is now admiring the marks. He's certainly not going to apologize for choking her, just as she isn't sorry she faked passing out.

His skin has warmed her but her body temperature still feels uncomfortably low. She swivels her hips to rub against him and he pulls back to look down the length of her pale flesh. Antal then grabs the back of each of Tó's knees to raise and press them up by her shoulders. Now she's stretched wide open and without any caresses he enters her hole with a powerful thrust. She's dry and it's painful but he pulls back only to roughly drive deep inside again. Since her hands are free Tó using one to pinch her nipples while the other strums her clit. His eyes move from watching what each one of her hands is doing, looking back and forth. This is one of those times when he likes to watch her play.

Touching herself helps and Tó feels some lubrication easing Antal's fucking. His grunt sounds approving so she continues at a faster pace. Just before she cums he releases his hold on her knees and pulls both her hands away. Stopping just on the verge makes Tó whine while Antal explodes inside her before collapsing and pinning her down with his full weight. He's so much heavier she can't even squirm to rub herself against his pelvic bone. Her hands are trapped, too.

Tó huffs in frustration but Antal simply chuckles. He rests his head on the pillow and uses his body to secure her from head to toe. By the time Tó's arousal has subsided Antal has fallen asleep. She restrains the urge to bite down on the soft hollow between his shoulder and neck.

Despite her discomfort Tó's eyes close and she naps until hunger wakes her. The bedroom is dark and she's alone. She heads downstairs in search of food. The dining-room is empty and tidy, as is the kitchen. There's no evidence Antal has eaten.

Tó makes herself toast which she spreads thickly with peanut butter. Carrying her plate she heads to the library and curling up in her favorite seat is soon immersed in a story and eating mechanically.

A couple of hours later Antal and Grigor burst into the room, startling Tó. They're wild-eyed, sweaty, and sniffing. Tó isn't in heat but she still carries a scent of her own the two men use to track her down.

Looking closely Tó spots smears of blood streaking across Antal's cheeks into his hairline and more flecks in his hair. Grigor is equally marked and she realizes they've been out as wolves chasing down prey.

Whatever angered Antal earlier drove him to first punish her with the choking, then to shift for a successful hunt, but she can see that his aggression still hasn't been assuaged.

In silent agreement both Antal and Grigor stalk towards her and Tó realizes that she is to be their victim now. Her heart pounds and she's sure the predator in Antal will hungrily spot the rapid pulse fluttering in her throat.

She isn't in heat and having these big, strong men run a train on her is going to hurt but... Tó will enter her own head-space to get through the pain and she will take their abuse of her body without begging for mercy. Her Alpha and Beta will sate themselves and afterwards will smother her with affection and appreciation, admiring her strength.

Antal is a well-built man who is big, whereas Grigor is mammoth. He's over six-and-a-half feet tall with powerful shoulders, thick arms, and a huge chest. His devotion to Antal extends beyond a Beta to his Alpha, Grigor loves Antal.

Wolf-shifters are naturally bisexual but Tó knows that Grigor's feelings run deeper than eroticism. She's been aware of that since the first time she saw them together. Her self-preserving instincts convinced her he isn't jealous or resentful so she's in no danger of him harming her intentionally. But there are always bruises and sometimes tearing when such a big man penetrates a slender girl.

They all have their roles and this is a part of the price she pays for their protection, and for the comfort of her home.

3

We had a translator come by for a couple of hours. Well, specifically he came to update the computers with new security and the surveillance system got overhauled and reinforced.

It seems someone's been trying to break into our system. They've been unsuccessful so far but, as Al explained, they only need to breach our defenses once and apparently they've been bombarding us with attempts. No wonder Antal and Grigor were so angry.

Al has now updated and upgraded us with even stronger protections. I couldn't care less about that stuff, I just liked having someone to talk to.

At the Club people only spoke at me, not to me, but at least I could understand the conversations I heard. One thing I discovered here is that loneliness really isolates you when you don't know what anyone's saying.

Security Tech Al is English-Hungarian bilingual and a nice guy. It was great to actually have a chat and I enjoyed it right up until I felt the death-glare from Antal. I frowned right back at him because seriously? Look at Al and then look in a mirror and then try to stop smirking. Like I said, Al is a nice guy and we all know what an insult that is if you're describing someone for a blind date.

But he did do something wonderful for me and Antal when he installed a language program that will teach me written and spoken Hungarian. I was on it for two hours this afternoon and I think I've got some aptitude or an ear or whatever they call it when you can pick up languages fairly easily.

Being on the run throughout my teens meant I have no school smarts but I read a lot and have learned so much that way. I know this interactive program will be great.

So between the gardening in the morning, an hour or so of reading, an afternoon with the language-learning app – and dropping everything to fit in Antal whenever he demands to have his appetites satisfied – my days are now full and I'm never bored.

Once I master speaking Hungarian I'll feel part of the conversations around me even if I don't participate directly. I can spy! Antal and I will be able to converse as well.

Al did me another favor when the safety program he installed in our cameras detected a threat and triggered an alarm moments before a car opened up on us outside in the garden in a drive-by shooting.

I didn't understand what was happening but when that siren shrieked I knew enough to flatten myself on the ground and drag the old gardener down with me. The thick bricks of the garden wall prevented the bullets from penetrating when the shooters sprayed their automatic

weapons. Only the top of the wall got chipped, but if we'd stayed standing we'd be dead.

We couldn't call the police because the alarm also brought our guards out firing. Somehow they incapacitated the vehicle, probably by killing the driver, and dragged another man into the house. He was taken to the basement and I never saw or heard anything about him again.

I did hear Antal and Grigor talking about the Fehers, a name I remembered hearing the three Alphas mention back in the Club. But of course I didn't ask for details.

The shooting was an awful thing to happen but strangely enough I'm not scared. I do feel safe and secure here. I guess it all happened too fast for me to really absorb any kind of bad feeling about it. I'm certainly not traumatized.

I guess my past has something to do with how easily I accept that shitty are going to happen and that we live surrounded by violence. I can't be frightened all the time. And maybe the overall improvement in my physical and mental health has given me sufficient stamina and confidence to better deal with the world's fuckery.

4

Two days after the shooting Antal hands me some clothes to put on, God knows where he got them - he threw out the stuff I'd brought - and takes me down to the garage. Grigor is waiting with a town car running.

I have no idea where we're going and trying to communicate with Antal is a struggle. I'm wearing baggy sweats and an oversized tee. Well, it's probably not oversized on its owner but... Anyhow, we're obviously not going anywhere fancy. Maybe I won't even be getting out of the car? But then why bring me?

"Are we going clothes shopping?" I ask feeling cute. Antal might not understand my words but he hears the underlying tone and scowls at me. He doesn't scare me quite as much as he used to but I'm smart enough to know when to shut up.

After driving for some time we end up in the countryside parking in a big lot outside a long low building. It's a shooting range and Antal is going to teach me how to shoot.

When he sees how excited I am he chuckles and says something in Hungarian to Grigor who just shakes his head, but I see his lips quirk in a smile through the rear-view mirror.

Once inside we wait while Grigor signs us in at a long counter that holds a variety of guns in the cabinet below. I don't have any ID but I don't need it, I'm not buying anything. Both he and Antal look at the various weapons with interest, obviously discussing the individual merits, when the man serving us calls out to someone in a back room.

Moments later a giant of a man, tattooed from the top of his shaved head right over every inch of exposed skin comes out with a greeting in halting Hungarian. He's Russian, as I later learn, and between the three of them they manage a conversation. The subject being me and what type of gun will suit.

Eventually we're led down a corridor passing a number of glassed-in booths. Some empty ones, but most are occupied by one or more people wearing large head-sets with protective ear coverings. Each booth faces down a deep room where the targets are hung.

Each door has to remain closed to maintain the soundproofing and there really isn't room for all of us. Finally Grigor and the Russian step out in the hallway and watch us through the window in the door. Of course we can't hear each other.

Antal is an experienced shooter so he gets me set up with the head-set and shows me how to stand and where to place my fingers but... I can't do it. I can't lift the gun, it's just too heavy. Even with two hands I can't hold it up never mind steady enough to aim and shoot.

Seeing the disappointment on my face, the Russian pops his head in to say he'll find something else for me. So Antal puts on his own head-set, picks up the weapon he chose, and proceeds to fire rapidly into the target each shot landing dead center and punching out a smooth hole.

He wields his skill with cool precision and it's pretty hot to watch him. He glances over to see me staring at him instead of the gun or the target and that makes him smirk. Arrogant, over-confident prick... but I'm rubbing my thighs together.

About ten minutes later the man returns with two smaller guns for me to try. One is impossible but the other seems likely until I hold it up. I can lift it but my grip is shaky and the gun wobbles all over the place. I've never felt so pathetically weak in my life and expect Antal to yell at me but he doesn't. In fact, he gives my shoulder a pat which I think is supposed to be consoling. It's not.

I step out into the corridor while Grigor comes in to take a turn. Both he and Antal are ace shots. It's good I have them to protect me. Physically I'm much stronger in my wolf form but I can hardly hold a gun with a paw.

Thoroughly dejected I follow the men out but the Russian stops us at the counter and speaks to Antal. He's points to a page in a catalog he's holding and Antal nods *yes* in answer to some question. Grigor steps up with a credit card to pay for whatever is being ordered but Antal stops him. He's spied a collection of knives hanging in a glass case on the opposite wall and hasn't finished shopping yet.

At first I'm reluctant to join him when he motions me over because who wants a stupid knife when there are guns on offer? But some protection is better than none so I take a look and the evil inside me lights up at all the wickedly sharp and shiny blades. If Antal's proficiency at the targets turned me on these deadly beauties have me salivating.

They come in so many shapes and styles and sizes. Antal points to a couple and hefts them in his hand when the man brings them out. Then he twirls the open blade through his fingers and I'm mesmerized. I want to learn how to do that. I'm sure I can do amazing things if I practice lots.

When he finishes showing off he's studying me with one eyebrow raised and I grin back at him. Oh yeah, he knows I'm his psycho girl. He lets me pick out a few knives to hold and I finally settle on one with a bone handle. It's not the prettiest but it seems to call to me. It comes with a forearm sheath for easy concealed carry. The one Antal chooses for himself has a thinner blade with a wicked curve.

When our purchases are bagged the Russian tells me my gun should be here within three or four days and when I look puzzled he opens the

catalog page to show me a tiny gun, called a Lady Derringer, that Antal
has ordered for me. It's so beautiful! I squeal with delight and throw
my arms around my man but he pushes me away and tries to look stern.
Grigor is grinning like a fool.

"Thank you so much for my gun and my knife, Antal, I love them both,"
I say happily.

He exchanges a few words with the Russian who gives a surprised burst
of laughter before enunciating slowly:

"You will learn to love my knife, too."

Antal repeats the words back to him and then turns to me saying them
again. I have no idea what he's talking about, but as soon as we get
home I find out.

We enter the house through the garage but instead of leading me to the
stairs Antal stops, looking down the room where I see there's another
door. Something ancient in my DNA warns me to keep absolutely still.
Like a rabbit frozen in fear or... self-defense.

Antal turns to look at me and my insides go icy cold. It's like he's no
longer inhabiting his body but instead has given over the space to a
demon. His demon. The eyes that look back at me are merely pupils
and solid black. His face has become a mask and his aura is bloody.

The sound of Grigor's steps coming towards us breaks the spell and I'm
ready to run in the opposite direction but Antal snags hold of my wrist,
tight, and draws me close. His hand cups my chin and tilts my face
upwards. He stares into my eyes and I hear him draw in a deep breath
before whispering *Tö* in a gusty exhalation.

Grigor has sensed something's wrong and he moves to stand on the far
side of Antal herding him towards the stairs. I try to lead him that way

too but my legs are shaky and stiff. I'm almost paralyzed by my fear. I realize that far door leads to the dungeon and I do not want Antal to take me there. Ever.

Looking into my eyes seemed to ground him so I force myself to look up and gaze at him. He swings me up in his arms and carries me, bride-like, up the stairs with the two of us staring at each other for every step.

Being this close I can see the pulse pounding in his temple and hear him grinding his teeth. His inner devil is hungry and angry at being thwarted. This isn't going to be an easy night for me. I need to keep my wits about me, control any panic, and play this cleverly.

Much later I lie awake while Antal sleeps so deeply he might be unconscious. The sheets are soaked and my skin is damp with – literally – blood, sweat, and tears. I feel boneless, certainly too exhausted to get up and wash. Wrung out emotionally, mentally, physically I can only lie here replaying the activities I experienced in this bed tonight.

Replay, play – those are the key words. By treating everything as a game of role-playing I was able to participate well enough to feed the urges of Antal's demon and survive the ordeal. I can't control the shudder that passes through me when I remember the curved blade on that knife he bought. It's so sharp, so wickedly, cruelly sharp.

Antal tied me to his bed posts but propped up with pillows so I was reclining against the headboard. He wanted me to have a clear view. First he sliced the too-big clothing from me. It was ugly so I didn't mind the loss, but seeing that knife so close to my skin and me bound and helpless was frightening. And yet I felt a primal heat in my core and knew my heavy breathing wasn't just from fear. The knife separated the material effortlessly and my nipples had pebbled by time he removed every scrap. My thighs were trembling when he sliced the sweatpants off of me.

Tossing the remnants aside Antal stroked my body a few times with his hands before running the knife along my skin. I immediately got goosebumps and that gave him the idea to cool off the blade in the ice-bucket on the drinks cabinet. He only swirled it around the cubes a few times but it was enough to make me gasp at the icy burn.

The coldness numbed my skin so much that I didn't realize he'd actually cut me until I saw thin rivulets of blood stream down the front of me. He used the knife to trap a few of the drops then gathering them on the blade he lifted it to his mouth and licked. He cut his tongue mingling his blood with mine. Then he kissed me.

The scratches were as superficial as a kitten's claw marks or a paper cut but they hurt.

He continued crisscrossing the knife over my flesh, usually just scoring a bloodless line but occasionally his angle was too acute and beads of blood formed. Each time that happened he would lap it up.

Soon his lips were stained red and mine must have been as well since he kept kissing me. I felt utterly terrorized but something warned me to play it up so I shivered and moaned, oohed and aahed and if he heard my teeth chatter he only thought I acted the part well.

Every time the blade touched my skin I held my breath and stayed motionless. When Antal dragged the edge down to my pussy I almost convulsed in a panic but instead made some comment about me preferring his dick and he settled for tapping the metal against my clit and slicing off a curl of my white-blonde pubic hair.

By then I was covered in a sheen of sweat and he must have known I was frightened but trying to hide it. He let me pretend.

Despite my ordeal I can't deny I was aroused. I don't know why or how I ever got to be fucked up enough to have that kind of reaction but he smelled me, he stuck his nose right into me and sniffed deeply. Then he tossed the knife down beside me and fucked my blood-streaked body with violence. He struggled to flip me over before remembering my hands were tied. Grabbing up the knife he freed me with two slashes to the rope before taking me doggie-style and pounding so deep inside.

I'd like to believe that I hated every minute but my orgasms were truly mind-blowing. The waves of pleasure hit like a tsunami and I think I passed out for awhile. I know my throat was hoarse from crying out his name and his voice echoed *Tŏ! Tŏ! Tŏ!*

Now I'm trying to blank my mind so I can cling to my sanity. I've already given up on trying to hang on to my sassy self.

5

Antal knows I'm watching even though he doesn't acknowledge me. Am I about to get another lesson? Or does this little exhibition have nothing to do with me? He likes to keep me guessing. He likes me as an audience, just as he likes watching me.

The woman is all over him. Obviously they've been together before because now she's acting like she owns him or something. The possessive type. She really doesn't know him all that well.

Voluptuous is the only way to describe this woman although in ten years – maybe less – the adjective will be overblown. For now she's got dusky skin, long black hair, dark eyes and a killer body. Enormous tits, way bigger than Mandy and Marcie's natural Cs but... I realize I don't have to think about them anymore. They're dead and their breasts are nothing now. I pause to consider whether or not I care about that and realize that nope, I don't give a shit.

Antal's English is coming along well because he really wants to learn so we work at it a lot. Plus, as a runty Omega, I never had much to do but live in my book world with my book friends. Reading is the best way to learn and if I don't know how to pronounce some of the words properly well... who's going to know? Turns out I'm a good teacher.

Strip is one of the words he learned quickly and easily. The woman hastens to comply even if she does try to act coy with her licked lip come-ons, and cutesy-oopsy expressions.

I'm rolling my eyes so hard you'd think someone was actually watching me but that isn't happening, not with Miss Triple Ds in the room.

He doesn't give her a chance to show off her seductive, lacy lingerie but it got my attention. When she tries to pose he just gestures for her to hurry up and get it off. I can't help smiling a little, probably because I'm so jealous of how well she fills it. She looks so sexy.

Soon she's naked and bent over his desk. He gets into position to take her from behind, gripping her by her breasts. They're so huge they overflow even his big hands. Can they possibly be real? He squeezes roughly and I think to myself *he's mauling the girl. She's going to have red fingermarks, probably even bruises, by time he's done.*

Keeping his clothes on Antal unzips and immediately plunges inside with no foreplay. That's gotta hurt, I know how big his cock is. He alternates each thrust with a hard smack on her ass, hitting from the softest fullest spot upwards. Thrust then spank but only on her right cheek which is getting redder and redder. I see that her teeth are gritted tight despite the oohing and groaning sounds of pleasure she's making. I'm pretty sure she's faking her enjoyment which is such a waste with a man like him. Unless she's a pain-slut?

Antal doesn't wait long enough to find out. He finishes quickly then tucks his dick back into his pants. He turns her around so she's sitting on the desk and from my vantage point I can see that one cheek is bright red. Antal doesn't look at her face. His focus in on her tits and he's twisting her nipples hard while she struggles not to cry out.

He moves from her nipples to slap the open palm of his right hand across her left breast then comes back with his left hand hitting her right breast. Striking her almost lazily, certainly without any expression or emotion on his devilishly handsome face. Back and forth, one hand then the other, heavy breasts shaking and the skin turning pink. He's spanking her tits! Once she loses control and begins sobbing deeply he loses interest. Walking away from her he comes towards me and pull me into his embrace. The two of us stand in the doorway silently watching. Her eyes track him and now she sees me. With tears streaming down her face from both the pain and the humiliation the woman gathers up her clothes and dressing quickly leaves without a word. *Strip* is the only thing Antal has said from start to finish. He's a vicious man who likes to demean and degrade these larger-than-life women. She isn't the first he's used to put on a show for an audience of me. I hope he pays them well.

As usual I'm dressed in one of Antal's dress shirts with nothing underneath. I don't button up, instead I wrap a sash around my waist and he likes to get me naked simply by tugging on it. Each day I put on the shirt he discarded the previous night. He likes to see me in his clothes and I like to be wrapped in his scent.

Now that I'm being properly fed my body has begun to fill out. My breasts are only marginally bigger then before, and I still wear an A cup, but my ass is now big enough to pinch... a little bit.

Anatomy was the subject of our first English lesson. I pointed to our various body parts and told him the names. All the names from vagina to pussy to snatch to cunt; penis, dick, schlong, and cock; bosoms, breasts, boobs, and tits. Also the parts of the face and it turns out he loves my aquamarine eyes. Also my mouth, lips, and tongue. He's eyeing them now but no way am I sucking his dick after he's stuck it in her.

I say shower first, then you can fuck my mouth and he narrows his eyes as if that will scare me. I'm pretty sure Antal knows I already live in a constant state of terror. Why wouldn't I? I live with a psychopath or sociopath or whatever the right name is for someone who does what he wants, when he wants, and how he wants. And those wants of his usually involve somebody else's pain.

He's considering my words and trying to decide whether or not to just force his dick into my mouth right now or to punish me. When I'm disobedient he'll sit me in his lap and spread my legs, exposing me and tormenting me to the very edge again and again until I'm soaking and writhing and begging for release. Although he spanked that woman, or at least one of her butt cheeks, spanking really isn't his thing. Maybe he's afraid of hurting me or maybe my bum's too bony to appeal and I'm glad!

Degradation and shaming me, preferably publicly, is his choice of punishment. Too bad for him that he doesn't really humiliate me because I couldn't care less what people think or say. I've been living on borrowed time ever since I witnessed the cold-blooded murder of three people not five feet away from me. People I hated, true, but that should be beside the point. At least I think I should feel that way.

If I refuse to do something that he thinks is good for me like eating, sleeping, or exercising, I get two spanks to punctuate each word in the phrases *eat more* and *sleep now* or *walk outside.*

That doesn't sound like much but two swats are ample punishment since his big hand covers both my ass cheeks and he hits hard, leaving me with a stinging bottom. Sitting around reading when I should be taking a walk in the fresh air is my most common transgression. I never see him read and I think he's jealous of how books, or rather my eReader, grab hold of my attention.

He's flogged me and whipped me but lightly compared to what I've seen him do to his lovers. And he doesn't just whip their asses when he wields the leather. Unfortunately for the women the more luscious their bodies are the more likely he is to treat them cruelly. I have no idea why he suffers this kink and I certainly have no intention of asking.

If he ever offers to buy me a boob job I'm going to refuse, if I can.

I've been living here with Antal for a few months, I think. I have very little access to the outside world and can only judge time by the changes to the weather and the work I do with the plants within the walled garden. I'm expected to be out for a walk around the lawn every day and I've noticed that the weather has turned colder. It must be Fall now.

Sometimes I feel like one of the falling leaves being blown here, there, and everywhere by a capricious wind with no ability to control the direction I'm being taken. Antal is like the cat that frolics in play with the leaf before slamming down its paw to capture and bite it.

While I've let my mind cycle through all these thoughts and recollections his eyes have simply grown colder as he stares at me and through me. I give him a slow blink, hoping this sign of submission will distract him but no, it's only focused his growing rage.

I don't care, I'm not sucking a dick that's been inside someone else's pussy.

Without warning I shift into my wolf form and race away. After only a split-second's pause I hear him pounding after me. I head for the staircase to go up to the bedroom.

He'd once told me the basement was off-limits. At the time I didn't really understand what he said but a messenger was waiting for Antal in the hallway and hearing our conversation he translated for us. A somewhat rough translation that sounded like blood-letting play in the dungeon and I screeched blood PLAY? not understanding what that entailed, but he didn't elaborate. Just nodded and said hurt bad, many blood. Turning back to Antal I caught him eyeing me with a speculative look and I knew I needed to distract him from whatever he was thinking. I was sure his thoughts involved play for him but hurt and blood for me.

Our language lessons had been coming along so I pressed my body against his and gazing at him wide-eyed I said: "No dungeon for Tó, Tó is Antal's jó kislány (good girl)," and tried for a winsome smile.

He gave me his unblinking stare that means he's still thinking. I pulled my shirt open to bare one breast and then lightly traced it like a blind person would. Gently feeling my way all around the nipple which puckered and tightened and darkened, showing its craving. Antal's eyes were locked on my fingers which came close to my nipple but never actually touched it. He lifted his gaze to meet mine and I gave him my best submissive *please-give-me-permission* look.

Suddenly he scooped me up in his arms then lowered his head to nip, nibble, and suck my nipple. That started the other one aching for his mouth. I guess I sent that thought telepathically because he used his teeth to pull the shirt fully open. He licked and kissed and lightly bit both of my small breasts with their hard deep-pink nipples. A full day's growth of beard made his chin rough and he left red, abrading marks across my chest. I reached up to stroke his shoulders then drag my fingers up his neck through his hair along his scalp. He made approving noises so I dared to lean forward and kiss his cheek.

Pulling his head back he once again stared deeply into my eyes, but I had no clue what he was thinking. Then he turned his head aside and dismissed the bilingual messenger who I had totally forgotten was there, waiting and watching us.

A full day's growth of beard makes his chin rough and he leaves red, abrading marks across my chest. I reach up and stroke his shoulders then drag my fingers up his neck through his hair along his scalp. He makes approving noises so I dare to lean forward and kiss his cheek. Pulling his head back he once again stares deeply into my eyes, but I haven't a clue what he's thinking.

Then he turns his head aside and dismisses the bilingual messenger who I had totally forgotten.

I remember all this as I'm racing away from him, knowing I have to head up the stairs, and hoping I can reach our bedroom before he pounces. We both know he's going to catch me but I'd like to be out of the hallway – at least off of the stairs – before I'm captured and claimed. I know he won't hesitate at the thought of being seen by the servants and, I'm ashamed to say, their presence won't hold me back either. But when I next have to face them in discussions over mundane tasks my cheeks will be burning at the memory. Not from shame but arousal as I suspect they know! I've become an exhibitionist and they've all seen us at it before.

Running as a wolf is exhilarating. I can only imagine what it would be like outdoors, in the woods, in the dark... I dream about it.

I dream about running with a pack, with a mate, being chased by a mate and being caught by him. A victory for both of us but first the heart-pounding, ice-in-the-veins dread of having to flee, to escape. The thrill of being pursued and hunted down. Paying the penalty of capture. Complete surrender: both of us with heaving chests, blood running hot, and panting hard. His to claim, mine to tame. We rarely go out but I hope we can experience that some day.

My she-wolf is slight in build so I'm able to take the corners and curves quickly where Antal's big Alpha crashes into walls, but then he's strong enough to push off those same walls to gain ground. I have to rely on my speed and agility to get me up that winding staircase ahead of him.

I did it without getting caught! He'd have ravaged me for sure and when I'm not in heat being taken in wolf form can really hurt. Especially when he's in a biting mood. Now I scurry to my destination to shift and await my master.

I hear him come crashing down the hallway then bursting through the bedroom door but I'm not in that room. I'm in the shower, the waterfall showerhead raining down on me as I kneel naked and waiting. Utterly submissive, obedient and vulnerable. Just as he likes me.

The door slams against the wall and there he is, shifting into a steaming, red-faced man being led by his hard cock. I reach out my hands to invite him close and when he steps in the shower I immediately begin soaping his balls and stroking the whole length of his shaft with a soft washcloth. Once the stink of that woman is off him my mouth makes love to his dick with everything I've got.

I take my time, I gently touch and tickle, I feather him all over with kisses, I lick and I suck until he demands more. His balls tighten as he grabs my jaw and holding my mouth open and steady he proceeds to fuck it. Angrily stroking hard and deep. Hitting the back of my throat to make me choke, filling me up until I gasp for air, my eyes are swimming in tears when I meet his gaze. His seem to be nothing but black pupil and I know mine are brightly shimmering aquamarine. We're locked on to one another and I think he's as mesmerized as I am, he truly does love the color of my eyes. Maybe he's never seen anything like them before?

He's still holding my head firmly in place to force me to swallow when he cums down my throat. I'm expecting that so I do so without gagging although saliva streams from the corners of my mouth. Finally his features soften into something that is almost a smile.

"Tó is Antal's good girl," he says, and I nod eagerly. Picking up the washcloth and soap I work my way down one muscular thigh and calf right down to his foot. He lifts it while I carefully wash all over including between his toes. After using the cloth to rinse I bend right down and suck on his big toe for a moment before planting a loud smacking kiss. Then I move onto his other foot and perform the same ritual in reverse order.

As I reach his groin I slide my hands around to soap his backside. He has a tight butt with surprisingly soft skin. I slide the soap right down the crack of his ass to play it around the puckered rim of his anus. Pressing there gently I rub my cheek against his semi-hard dick. It's time to give over control to let him decide if I've earned an orgasm or if he needs to punish me with denial.

He pushes me so I fall back and I recline on my elbows on the tiled floor. He motions me to spread my legs and I obey promptly. Scooting down to a crouch he eyes me from head to toe. There are only a couple of scratches left from his knife play and they'll soon disappear. I never used to be a fast healer, I was always sickly, but I feel strong and healthy now. Maybe it has something to do with me freeing my Omega nature?

Antal has a good look inside the gaping lips of my vagina and despite my efforts to wait patiently I can feel my clit twitching under his gaze, signaling my arousal. When he looks in my eyes I'm happy to show him the desire I feel.

He flicks my clit and a shock of pain and excitement stings me. That little bundle of nerve endings has fully awakened to him and if he makes me wait another minute I'm going to start begging.

He stands up abruptly, grabbing my wrist and yanking me upright along with him. Tucking me under his arm he carries me – both of us soaking wet – to the big bed and tosses me in the middle of it. He's immediately on top of me, hungry and demanding, hands roving everywhere and roughly grabbing. Asserting his authority over me. Claiming me and fucking me hard.

I can never get enough of this man.

6

Kartal has come to visit us with a message – a warning – from Sandor in Hungary. The Fehers have upped the ante and are suspected in several attacks with one ending in a fatality.

Sandor has a second family with his younger wife and the school their children attend was bombed. Fortunately no children were injured because the bomb went off almost an hour after school had let out for the day, but one of the caretakers died.

The police declared it a terrorist attack since the children of several prominent politicians attend that school, but Sandor is convinced the Fehers were behind it.

Antal talks about his household being under surveillance, and says his guards have noticed watchers on several occasions. When he goes out his car is always followed. This is news to me. Then he mentions the drive-by shooting and I am thankful once again for the warning alarm installed by Al the security guy.

Antal suspects it is the Feher gang and Kartal nods in agreement. Kartal goes on to explain that Sandor doesn't feel he can safely leave his family right now so he instructed his Beta to visit with Janos to try to convince him to travel to meet with Antal in America. He's obviously proud to represent his clan this way.

Kartal reports that Janos said he doesn't want to leave his family or businesses right now either. There have been hijackings of trucks carrying shipments for him, a warehouse mysteriously burned down, and a number of other small but annoying and expensive problems have occurred. Too many for random acts of violence or vandalism from disgruntled employees.

Also, he can't visit Antal so long as he's got Tó with him. There was a major blow-out with his Erzsébet over Janos' infidelity, and he was forced to assert his authority several times. She gets violent in her jealousy. Things were uneasily settled until Kartal arrived and re-awoke all the animosity Erzsébet was feeling. She publicly berated and insulted Janos and that called for punishment.

As a sudden silence descends Erzsébet knows she's gone too far, spoken too loudly, and been too insulting. Although her connection with Janos, her fated mate, runs deeper than that of most couples, to the rest of the pack he is the Alpha and she has disrespected him. Publicly. Now she has to be chastised... publicly.

She beseeches him with a pleading look of remorse but the cold gaze Janos returns is that of an uncaring stranger. He has a cruel streak and an icy shiver of trepidation and fear runs through Erzsébet.

At his signal, two men grab her by the arms and drag her over to the punishment post at the top of the room where everyone present had a clear view of her wrists being secured to the leather cuffs. With her arms pulled above her head her cheek is forced against the rough wood.

Janos is visibly struggling to control his rage as he stalks up and taking hold of the collar of her dress slices right through the material with a hunting knife, all the way down to the hem. He's also cut through her undergarment leaving Erzsébet naked and exposed.

Erzsébet feels the cool air on her skin but her shivering is from dread rather than cold. The goosebumping she experiences is in anticipation of the harsh correction her wrathful Alpha will inflict and she hopes she can deal with the pain with some dignity. Hearing the whispering sound of Janos's belt being whipped from its loops and whistling through the air she cringes against his anger, knowing she'll soon be giving in to the most undignified screams.

"He belted her in front of everyone?" gasps Tó in horror.

"Yes of course, he had to do so, you know how it goes."

"Had to? No! I certainly don't know..." she's aghast.

Kartal looks to Antal who explains that Tó was abandoned by her pack soon after birth and she knows nothing of clan traditions or pack behavior and expectations.

"Oh! Well, when an offence calls for corporal punishment it must be administered publicly and witnessed by the pack. That's justice. The miscreant is whipped with a leather belt – shoulders to waist for men and waist to knees for women – with a welting only on the buttocks for boys and girls," Kartal told her.

"Boys and girls?"

"Yes, they get two strokes but only for dangerous naughtiness like lighting fires. The public humiliation is the key. Actually, it's not so much humiliation but submission to the will of the pack for the good of the pack. Pack loyalty and unity is everything. Obedience is the key."

He's been speaking bilingually to both Antal and Tó. Now he adds: "You'll understand better when you join a pack yourself–"

Antal interrupts to say: "That's not going to happen. Ever. I have been banished from my pack due to unsanctioned and uncontrollable violence – at least that's what they claimed – and Tó is mine, she will always be staying with me."

"Ahh. Well, Erzsébet received a brutal belting from Janos and while the she-wolves all sympathized with her painful welts everyone, male and female alike, caught the strong scent of her arousal. Again, following the traditional discipline for a mate, Janos then um... had intercourse, before Erzsébet was let down from the post."

"You mean he fucked her from behind while she was tied up, in front of everyone, after savagely beating her?"

"Well, yes, I guess you could put it that way. He wasn't really savage though, no I would say more cold and calculating. He took his time between each stroke to lay it in the position he wanted. Her stripes were perfectly even and then he slashed diagonally across her bottom in one direction and then in the other direction across her thighs. It was artistry. Then he flung his belt aside, withdrew his cock and yeah, fucked her."

Tó screws up her face in disgust but Kartal hastens to add: "Her screams of pleasure were far louder than her shrieks of pain. Truly. And when Janos finished with her the whole room erupted in applause and the pounding of tables with people holding out their drinks and shouting a toast to their Pack Queen. They all admired the way she took the dozen lashings their Alpha gave her, and cheered her lusty response to his mating. Everyone is hopeful for an heir."

Antal takes hold of Tó's chin and tilts her face up until they've locked into each other's eyes. He speaks and Kartal interprets for him saying:

"We have no pack but I'd like to discipline you in front of our entourage. I think only four strokes for you. I'm more interested in discovering what your subsequent response will be."

"I'll hate it!" declares Tó, but Kartal tells her that her body will definitely demand to be sated.

"It is simply a condition of she-wolves," Kartal says with a shrug. "A degree of pain adds spice to their arousal. The men dominate their mates with spankings or beltings and the females accept and submit. Erzsébet has a high pain threshold and a strong libido.

When I reported back to my Alpha both he and his lady laughed at the story saying Erzsébet's jealous temper is well-known and this wasn't the first time Janos has had to discipline his mate in front of their pack."

Tó frowns at Antal but that only makes him smile, a smile that soon turns into the very aptly named wolfish grin. She turns back to Kartal who struggles to keep up with the translation as Antal speaks rapidly in an urgent tone.

"He wants me to lift up your shirt and–"

"Strip, strip!" commands Antal.

"I'm trying to teach him English," says Tó, "but he has a selective vocabulary."

She stands up to remove her lover's shirt, giving Antal a wary look. As usual when she's naked his eyes rake over her from head to toe.

He continues speaking to Kartal who tells Tó: "He wants me to have a good look at your ass and confirm that it is um... plumping out?"

"Filling out?"

"Yes, that must be it. And yes, your backside is filling out from what I uh... um, remember from last time when you were–"

"In heat and we fucked a few times. Yeah, I remember that much and it was probably great, but unfortunately that time is a blur. All my heats are, I've had some more since then. I guess I go into heat about every three-and-half weeks and will do so until I conceive."

"Oh, is that the plan?"

"God, no!" she shudders.

"Antal wants to know what we're talking about."

"Go ahead and tell him the truth, he already knows and agrees, neither one of us is parent material."

Antal laughs loudly then gives Kartal a lengthy explanation.

"You're right, he agrees no pregnancy. He doesn't want to share your body with a baby, only with a few male friends. Or maybe even females if he finds some who will play with your toys. Oh... now he's saying he definitely wants that to happen at your next heat."

"I'll bet he does," grumbles Tó. "In fact, I bet he counts off the days on a calendar."

Kartal chuckles at her grumpy expression then, after listening some more, continues imparting Antal's conversation:

"He's asking if I think you're filling out all over and yes, you are. Your um... backside, as I mentioned is definitely nice and round. It used to be just muscle with no fat but now," he reaches out to cup her cheeks but pauses, looking to Antal for permission first. At the Alpha's *yes, yes* gesture Kartal gives her bottom a squeeze and an appreciative caress. "This is nice, a least half-a-handful of soft flesh."

"Uh, thanks?"

"Oh, sorry Tó. I get like this when I'm around an Alpha. Okay, now I've got to turn you around and check out the front of you. Hmm, no belly yet and your hipbones still stick out but there's a curve to your hips that's new," he says, running his hands from her thighs up to her waist. "I think overall there's a little more padding although I can still feel your ribs. Your breasts might be a little bit fuller, but I can't be sure. You're not absolutely flat," he assures her.

Tó shakes her head but with a smile. Antal couldn't care less about what cup size she wears, he just likes to twist and pinch her nipples. She enjoys that as well. The pleasurable sensation makes her pussy clench in a way that far outweighs the discomfort of his roughness.

All this sexual talk and touching has aroused Kartal. Antal notices and laughing tells the young man to go ahead and help himself.

"Tó, um Antal is telling me to... to uh, um..."

She understands and gets down on all fours then drops her forearms flat on the carpet, lifting her hips and spreading her legs so that her pussy is fully exposed and accessible. Kartal quickly pulls his pants down and guides his hard cock inside her.

Tó has locked her gaze with Antal's and the two stare at each other, unblinking, while she gets fucked. Antal, practising his English, instructs Kartal to *rub clit*. His eager touch brings Tó to orgasm and Antal nods with satisfaction. Kartal continues pumping and rubbing and this time he joins in her second climax.

Afterwards Antal motions to Tó to leave him and Kartal alone to talk. As she picks up her shirt Kartal tells her: "He says to stay naked, wait on the bed, and don't clean yourself of my.. um, cum."

Tó nods then says goodnight to Kartal. Unspoken between them is the knowledge that Antal might still send the young Beta to Tó's bed tonight.

7

Both women smile widely at me, in fact they're grinning, and that feels a bit off. I'm leery of anybody who looks at me like I'm delicious.

They are beautiful themselves. Not Antal's usual type but well-built all the same. Tall brunettes with a strong hint of red in their hair. One wears hers very short, the other chin-length. Long-limbed they both tower over me.

"But she's perfect!" coos short hair.

"Ethereal, like something out of a fairytale," exclaims chin-length.

"So pale and slender and delicate..."

"And fragile and frail."

They're just speaking to each other because they're talking in English so Antal doesn't understand, and they're talking about me, not to me. It's like I'm not even in the room. I think that's pretty rude so when short hair starts rhapsodizing about my gorgeous eyes I close them. I can be rude too.

"Oh that's just delightful!" shrieks one of them. I don't know which because I can't see and they both sound the same.

"It will be such a pleasure to teach this naughty girl a lesson or two!"

Even though they can't tell I'm still gonna roll my eyes at that remark. I mean seriously, they're going to teach me manners? That won't be an issue.

I've figured out why they're here crooning over me and it isn't to paint my portrait. No, it's because Antal wants to see me played with by women in my next heat. Which, FML, is happening soon.

These humans have obviously never experienced a she-wolf in heat. They're the ones who will be learning plenty. I hope they have lots of stamina. I open my eyes and wink but when short hair reaches out to stroke my cheek I snarl and she jumps back.

Quick as a flash Antal has grabbed hold of me growling:

"*Nincs* [spank!] *harapás* [spank!] *(no biting)*."

I desperately want to rub the sting out of my bottom but I won't give him or them the satisfaction.

He exchanges a few sentences with chin-length hair in Hungarian which she translates for her companion.

"He says she edgy because she's very close. We might be back here as soon as tomorrow. I told him she must be restrained and he simply wants to know if we'll bring our own ropes and harness or do we want to use his? Isn't that delightful?"

"I'm shivering with pleasure."

"Me, too."

They both show me their eager, hungry smiles but I'm thinking my teeth can be much longer and sharper... but I'm willing to wait and see how well they do.

A few hours later I was overcome with the burning and the scent of my slick woke Antal. He fucked me twice then carried me into the living-room where four of his pack friends were already waiting.

We've all been here before and they know to play nice and share. The ones who are waiting their turn can play with their own cocks or each others. They will tire long before I do, and if everyone stays in their human form I'll come out of this mostly unscathed.

They immediately fall on my naked body grabbing and groping, pulling my legs wide apart and plunging right in. I love this! I feel dirty and depraved and oh-so-horny!

So now it's the next day and the two women are back. Olina, short hair, and Trudy, chin-length. They've brought along their own apparatus which they set up in the living-room as well. So here I am wearing a harness around my torso, suspended in mid-air, my wrists shackled to my ankles. All of the males are watching intently while these two females are laying out their toys.

Trudy flicks me lightly with a whip that doesn't cut me but does sting with each kiss of contact, enough to make me struggle. Olina is studying my cunt like she's having an anatomy lesson. At least that's how it seems until two pinches make me look down and I see that she's attached some clips to pin back my labia, leaving my clit completely unguarded. Ahh, that's the plan, I think as she produces a vibrator. *Bring it on!*

She buzzes it against me, changing the tempo with a turn of the dial and gauging my reaction. I'm soon bucking against my restraints and my poor clit is red and raw. The slick is dripping from me and I expect the men will soon be overcome by the attraction and the need to fuck me. I can't wait for them, I'm delirious with pleasure and want and need. The women don' t understand that all this foreplay is totally unnecessary. I just want to be fucked and I'm ready for it now. Oh well, let them fight it out amongst themselves so long as I get more, more, more.

I feel like I'm in a baby's swing as I'm lowered just enough to be fitted onto a hard cock. Fingers probe my back passage. The angle is wrong for entry and the guy who's got my cunt isn't willing to alter his position but that doesn't matter because only Antal is allowed to stick his dick in there. Other men, and women I guess, are allowed to poke with fingers and tongue and toys. While a man is rocking me by the hips one of the women slides a dildo inside me. Then she clips something against my clit and stepping back for a good view uses her phone to start both devices moving, wiggling, vibrating. It's diabolical and I love it!

I'm pretty much semi-conscious for the rest of the session. I knew there was an episode of hot wax making me writhe with pain and pleasure, and when I was released from the harness and cuffs my legs were like rubber. I end up over one of the women's knee being spanked with each smack in counterpoint to a thrust from the dildo being wielded by the other woman. Being led along so many creative paths to orgasm has been fucking fantastic.

Throughout it all I'm always aware of Antal's presence, watching the action and also watching over me. It's crazy to think what a relief it is to be relying on that psychopath's protection.

At one point I recall lying between Trudy and Olina, all of us naked, being soothed and petted with tender caresses. Yeah, no. I want to be used and abused by hard cocks. The women fall back, spent, while the strong sweet smell from my wet cunt draws a man-wolf to pound me.

Honestly they can't drive it in deep enough or rough enough or often enough. They all stoke their egos striving to satisfy my multi-orgasmic cunt even though they know my craving will be never-ending until the heat is over.

I am going to be really sore but post-heat always means a really deep, practically comatose, sleep that will give me time to heal. The only time

I stir is when Antal rouses me to drink a bottle of water. He holds me while I sleep it off. I guess the only time he can show me tenderness and affection is when I'm unconscious. He'll probably fuck me when I'm dead. I'll haunt him if he doesn't!

8

Kartal was a very active participant in my heat. Maybe he enjoyed the new curves that Antal's nourishment has brought? Or maybe he's become more familiar, and therefore more comfortable, with us and our unusual arrangement?

I do know it's unusual, but I don't know exactly what it is. I can't be a hostage, there's no one to send a ransom demand to, but I know I can't just walk out the front door so I'm definitely a prisoner of some sort. A prisoner of love? Ha! Hardly.

Antal treats me like a possession so I'm a... sex slave? a pet? an experiment? I'm certainly a captive, maybe all of the above? I don't spend a lot of time thinking about it because there's nothing I can do about it. And, let's be honest, sex prisoner and all, this is still the best life I've lived.

I've changed – mellowed – and I think maybe a lot of my prickly sarcasm was just me fighting the world, even if the world didn't know there was a battle being waged. Now I carry a lot less anger and a lot more fear. I mean, I'm not a quivering, cowering mess, well not often, but I don't kid myself about who and what my man is. I don't expect to have the chance to grow old.

Antal had a number of meetings and planning sessions with Kartal but those talks weren't translated for me. I was always present since Antal has taken to holding me naked in his lap all day long. He nuzzles my neck then casually teases my nipples and clit, keeping me in a constant state of arousal, and I squirm against his groin in retaliation while pressing down hard, trying to achieve some relief. That greatly amuses him. Eventually he'll indicate I can pull out his dick to suck him into readiness and then he'll fuck me.

Often he just keeps playing me to the very edge of climax and then pulls his hand away. Sometimes he lets me finish myself but more often he slaps my fingers and makes me suffer. He's trying to bring me to orgasm simply by blowing on my over-sensitized clit and damn if he isn't coming close.

The men always watch with interest but I notice that Grigor's eyes are on Kartal as much as me. I think he's jealous of the young Hungarian's relationship with Antal. As Beta's they're equals but Grigor is older and Kartal is a guest so the balance of power is in flux.

Kartal doesn't realize he's being used to stoke the flames of Grigor's possessive lust and love but I've let Antal see that I know what he's doing. He just smirks at me. He isn't capable of understanding Grigor's emotion, he just enjoys the added spice to the sex.

Kartal returned to Hungary without incident. Before leaving he assured me that Antal is taking the threat from the Feher family seriously, and has put protections in place. He mentions again what Antal told him about being watched and followed and assures me I'll be safe.

I'm sure I'll be fine because I'm never alone, and I never leave the property without Antal.

With Kartal gone Antal and I are back to struggling with pantomime and repetitive demonstrations to communicate. I manage to ask if he enjoyed seeing the women play with me and he indicates *yes* but shakes his head *no* when I ask if they'll be back next time. I'm not sure whose choice that is.

I miss having Kartal around and not just because of his English language skills. He's been in Sandor's clan since he was a boy so he knows a lot of the ins and outs of their organization and is willing to share. Antal used to be enforcer and no doubt was able to let off steam or get his kicks dealing with spies and traitors. Once he moved up his duties became more administrative.

The wolves only deal is armaments and have developed a sterling reputation in the underworld. Because they focus on guns they aren't involved in drugs or trafficking and won't allow anyone else to pursue either vice in their territory. That's why the Fehers want to break in.

Kartal tells Tó, "Sandor says the Fehers look down on us for being shifters instead of realizing we have evolved far beyond them. We don't enslave people to addictions and no one will steal girls out of our neighborhoods."

Antal let Kartal fuck me a few times and that was always pleasant but mostly it was just good to have someone else around as a buffer. Antal gets itchy or antsy or something for violence when he's got too much time to think. I suspect that inside his brain his thoughts writhe like snakes in a pit as they focus on bloody adventures: cutting, slicing, stabbing. Will I ever be proficient enough in Hungarian to understand? Assuming I could get him to tell me?

If his obsession-addiction-compulsion-whatever is jonesing him badly he settles it by bringing in one of his busty, beautiful girlfriends for sexual humiliation.

When the urges are very bad he disappears downstairs into the so-called dungeon and God only knows what he gets up to there. Although that's more likely to be the Devil's business. I never want to find out for myself. When he emerges with flecks of blood in his hair, soaked under his fingernails, and staining his chin my imagination becomes my own worst enemy. Well, probably my second worst enemy. I've known from the start my lover is a conscienceless predator.

I should probably try to escape and go to the police to report murderous goings-on but I'm not going to do that. I belong here, with him, and this is my world even though I didn't choose it.

For the first time in my life I get plenty to eat, I'm warm in my bed and can sleep comfortably, no one punches me just for breathing, and no one forces me to do drudge work when I'm so tired I can barely stand. If we are under surveillance then I guess I'm still in hiding but this time I have no fear of anyone other than the bogeyman I'm living with.

I'm twenty years old and I have absolutely no goals, no dreams, and no ambition. Just as well since I'm uneducated with no prospects. I'm not bitching, it is what it is. My life has been all about survival for the past seven or eight years. Now that I actually have a bed to sleep in I'm not doing anything to ruin that, Hell, I'll share it with Count Dracula. Oh wait, he was from Transylvania, so I guess I mean Vlad the Impaler. I'm pretty sure he was Hungarian.

There's no comparison between now and what my life was like back before the first killings of the Club Manager and the two Barbie lookalikes. I don't even remember their names but I do recall how they tormented me. Antal torments me too but in a pleasurable way. Mostly.

So sure, I know he's a killer and probably a torturer, and I figure I'm living on borrowed time but... it's a good time. For now.

9

Antal positioned me in the doorway so I'm standing in shadow but can be seen if someone looks hard enough. And I can see him and everything he's doing. He likes me as an audience but I have no idea why.

Is he showing off? Trying to make me jealous? Trying to make a point or teach me a lesson? If any of those questions are correct he's being too damn subtle for me.

This young woman is different. Oh she looks the same with her dark coloring and long wavy hair. Her killer body with its hourglass figure: humongous tits, and big round bum.

She's different in her attitude. He is an exceptionally handsome man and the other women were all panting for him but this one presents a challenge. She's definitely not a pushover... she's playing him like a pro.

The others seemed to know what to expect or at least how to behave but this one looks ready to make demands. My interest is definitely piqued and I can see that Antal's is as well. He's staring intensely, like he's intrigued by her.

She'd paused when she first came into the room but now she walks – struts – forward. As she draws close to him her hands drop to her hips and her pose clearly asks *like what you see?*

Making use of the one and only English lesson he really took to heart Antal commands: "Strip."

And the woman gives him a lazy half-smile while reaching for the buttons on her blouse. She works her way down slowly then tugging the tucked fabric from the waistband of her pencil skirt pulls the blouse wide open, showcasing phenomenal boobs barely contained in a lacy bra. She looks magnificent and I admit it: I'm jealous.

Shaking her left arm she frees it from the shirt sleeve then half-turns to pull the blouse off from the right and that's when I strike.

I'd never cover the distance from the doorway in time if I stayed in human form but my wiry wolf easily makes the leap. I crash into the woman, my jaws around her neck, and when she reflexively flings her arm up in protection the knife she's secreted goes flying.

Antal's reaction comes a split-second later and it's feral and vicious. He shifts as well, snapping and biting with his fearsome jaws. My bite tore her throat but wasn't strong enough to break her neck so she's still gurgling blood as she gasps to pull in air. The horror of her predicament is in her eyes and it spurs me on. She should never have messed with wolves.

I rip out her jugular then lap at the spray while Antal has bitten into her breasts. We both paw the soft body with our claws and growl appreciatively as we bite her all over. tearing out chunks of pale flesh.

We don't want to eat the body but it does feel good – really good, actually – to revel in the baseness of our natures to harm and hurt. Well, there's no more pain because the woman is dead but we still enjoy the mutilation.

Looking up I see my own blood-soaked muzzle reflected in Antal's black eyes. His jaws are dripping with saliva and blood and his curled lip shows his red-stained fangs. He growls, I snarl, and we simultaneously shift back into our human bodies which are vibrating with lusty arousal.

My passion for him is utterly overwhelming. I'm not in heat so I'm not producing my sweet-smelling slick to put him in rut, but he's burning up. His desire crackles like lightning in the air. Our mouths meet in a ravenous, consuming kiss that mingles the woman's hot blood on our lips.

We fuck and it's intense, my orgasm has me stuttering while his makes him howl. Then we make love and it's heartbreakingly tender, somehow my insides get twisted inside out and I'm just floating through the strobe-light flashing white spots under my eyelids.

We stare into each other's eyes and share a long, wordless moment. He rescued me from my old life and now that I've saved his we're even.

Antal will have to make the body disappear because a wolf-bitten corpse will attract too much negative attention. Nevertheless we need to pass on the message to the Fehers so I suggest he take photos on his phone to send to Sandor or Janos, or both of them. I also take the phone in order to get a picture of Antal bent over the body and smiling maliciously right into the camera. It's a scary-as-fuck shot. I get wet just looking at it.

Sometime no common language is a good thing. When we can only communicate in actions and not words we show our feelings clearly. Our black souls have called out to each other and now I'm here to stay.

Part Three

Once again my life has undergone changed circumstances. Saving Antal's life raised me in his eyes to... well, not an equal but to a cherished and pampered lover. I'm no longer treated like a pet doing tricks or a sex slave performing at his command. The sex, however, has gotten even better!

Antal still shares me but usually just with Grigor, and now he always participates in the play time. It's fantastic to be restrained against his massive chest, trapped by his muscular arms, while one of his friends holds my legs apart and licks me silly. Shifters have the most amazing growls when they're in human form aroused and enjoying themselves.

To have Antal growling in my ear, dangerously dragging his teeth up and down my throat is really hot but when you add in the growls of another man tormenting my clit with his tongue and his teeth... pure bliss!

With surprising patience Antal spent quite a bit of time introducing me to anal. Now he enjoys me that way often. I think my asshole would be used much more roughly if he hadn't discovered this new-found tenderness towards me as his savior. Thank God, because even after numerous sessions stretching me using lube, dildos, and butt-plugs his actual penetration is always still an ordeal. He's got a huge cock and I'm built small but it works out.

In fact, I've learned that if I relax I can enjoy it. That's going to take some more practice though, because I naturally tense up against the intrusion. But once he's actually inside it does feel good.

When his dick presses against what he explained, with help, is my PS-spot, the feeling is a really pleasant pressure. When he then starts rubbing my clit well... it's up and away for me!

Only Antal is allowed to partner me for anal sex. Our last session had a new twist with him taking my backdoor while his Beta, Grigor, took the front. That was.. indescribable wow. Feeling both dicks inside me at the same time with only... my womb, I guess? separating those two driving organs was exhilarating. Grigor was on his back with me lying flat on top of him, his dick buried deep and his hands spreading my butt-cheeks open. Antal pinned my wrists to the bed and skewered me in place via my ass.

I was held captive in the embrace of two very big, very strong men who shouted out words I couldn't understand in urgent tones. I orgasmed but they just kept pumping in counter-time to each other so every nerve-ending between my waist and knees was stimulated for every moment. When I climaxed a second time they joined in a hot, sticky explosion that soaked me.

Grigor dove between my legs to smear me all over with their cum, gently massaging it into my rubbed-raw holes simultaneously stinging and soothing both. Antal devoured my mouth with a soul-sucking kiss that kept me swept up in delirious delight. We were still breathing through each other's mouths when Grigor left us and Antal made love to me slowly, still engaged in that deep, satisfying kiss.

Later, he told me that he almost shot his load when he felt Grigor's cock moving inside me. He called to Grigor asking what he felt and Grigor replied *I feel like I'm fucking you, Alpha.* We'll definitely be enjoying simultaneous penetration again.

Antal still enjoys seeing me tied down and spreadeagled with a vibrator punishing my clit till I howl but no longer as the spectator. Now he's the one wielding the toy and when I'm tearful from the forced ecstasy it's Antal who fills me. I love being at his mercy, completely surrendered and submissive, and what I especially love is that he's now taking pleasure in my joy instead of my degradation. The changes in our relationship have all been good.

Although Grigor is only Antal's cousin he knows him better than the Szémozsa brothers do. He can read Antal's moods and knows how to distract or get him going. The smirk on his face as he follows Antal into the room this afternoon tells he's been shit-disturbing again.

"Tó, Grigor says you've been naughty and insists I give you a sound spanking."

"He does, does he? Well in that case he should be the one to administer the spanking."

"Yes, you're right, he should do it. He's got bigger hands that I do."

"But it's your job to discipline your mate, Alpha. As Beta my job is to punish the other women."

"What? What do you mean by that!?"

"You know, as Beta I'm in—"

"Grigor she has no clue about packs, remember? She grew up believing she's just a human and knows nothing of our lore."

"But surely... well okay, here goes. As Beta one of my duties is to chastise the unmated females in our pack. In this case, those in our compound here."

I don't like the sound of this but I know better than to voice my opinion until I've heard him out.

"How do you go about doing that?"

"Why by spanking them, how else?"

Antal wasn't kidding when he said Grigor has big hands. I look at them now and shudder at the thought of being chastised by him. He grabs up an iPad to bring up the Hungarian-English dictionary and after tapping a few times sets out to explain it to me.

"You don't understand yet, Omega, but she-wolves need a male's guidance for their physical and emotional well-being. We provide them with loving discipline—"

"Loving?"

"Yes, of course it is. Between a man and his mate it turns sexual - every time - but between a Beta and a female it's like a parent with their child."

"There's nothing childish about Maritsza when she's squirming bare-assed over your knee, Grigor," teases Antal.

"Oh Maritsza, that's different."

"Grigor! are you blushing?" I'm incredulous.

Antal joins me in ribbing the big man saying: "He thinks I don't know the truth about her but but Maritsza is his mate, he just needs to claim her."

"How can you tell?"

"Because they're both sexually aroused when he spanks her. He can smell her, not an Omega slick but her own female scent that calls to him. She wouldn't release this scent if I spanked her, only Grigor."

"I've heard of *fated mates*," I say wistfully.

"Maritsza and I aren't fated mates," Grigor insists.

"But it's true that when you spank her you both get horny and you fuck," points out Antal.

"You two fuck? Why don't you make her your mate?"

"Because Antal still needs my help with you and I'm not going to take a mate and then spend half my time having sex with you two."

"Grigor, you can't let me hold you back!" declares Antal, just as I say: "Do I know Maritsza? and would she like to join us?"

Both men look at me in surprise then commune silently with each other. Finally Grigor speaks telling me that Maritsza is the apprentice to our cook so no, I've never met her.

"Tell me about her, I bet she's pretty if she's your mate."

"She'd young, blonde, and fat," states Antal.

Grigor blushes again and it's adorable to see this huge, muscular hulking man acting shy. "Not fat—"

"As fat as a good cook should be. And with *nagy cicik (big tits),*" he demonstrates with his hands in front of his chest.

"Oooh, I'd like to see her and I'd like to touch her boobs," I say.

Thinking about that makes Antal start to hum. He tells Grigor: "Talk to Maritsza, let her know what you want. Do it soon, we want to know what she says."

"I will be seeing her soon because she gets sent for chastising a couple of times a week although I think Cook picks on her."

"Maybe the complaints are made at Maritsza's request," I say with a sly smile.

"Especially since you fuck her afterwards," adds Antal.

"Well, she wraps her arms around my neck to beg my forgiveness so it just kinda happens..." Grigor trails off as I chuckle.

I was hoping the turn the conversation took would make Antal forget his original comment but no such luck.

"So, back to Tó's punishment... like I said, spanking is so boring. There's no blood oh! I forgot about those paddles with embedded nails!" he exclaims.

"NAILS?" I shriek and Grigor chuckles.

"I can adjust the lengths, too." And I shiver because I see he's getting excited.

"Antal NO WAY will I submit to being paddled with nails, for fuck's sake. Just do NOT order something like that—"

"Oh I've already got one."

I give him a dirty look. He laughs when he notices adding: "Oh Tó, you and I know perfectly well what each of us likes. I know that you've found a way to escape into your head to transcend the pain and come out the other side finding pleasure."

There's nothing I can say to that because it's true. I just hadn't realized he'd figured it out.

"It still doesn't mean I want you to draw blood!" I retort. "Tó, Tó, Tó," he says shaking his head, "The best way to punish you, and my favorite method, is to deny you. I love to watch you when you're out of your head with desire but left unfulfilled.

The spectacle of you horny and sweaty, begging then swearing, promising and threatening, it's such a turn-on for me. I love to see you submissive and teary, trembling with need and swollen with lust.

Grigor, forget the spanking. Let's play with our girl by taking her right to the edge again and again."

"You still haven't opened that package you ordered, Alpha. It's sitting on the table by the front door. Should I get it?"

"Yes! Oh, yes. This will be fun!" Antal is enthusiastic about something that has me worried for my clit and my sanity. "Tó this will make you go crazy. It's a silicone massager with two heads to catch both sides of your clit. You're gonna hate it and I'll love it!'"

Grigor arrives with a small parcel and Antal sends him off to find a sling to help spread me, explaining: "We can use our hands more if we don't have to hold her legs open."

And so my torment begins. Antal decides he doesn't want me tied to the bed because then they won't be able to flip me around. He hooks the sling around my neck and attaches the cuffs to my ankles then secures my wrists to those same cuffs. My knees are pulled up to my chest and I'm fully exposed.

Now Antal tells Grigor to go wash the new toy and he gets me ready by drawing his tongue from my asshole right up to my clit. The sensation makes my butt clench involuntarily.

Grigor returns and Antal shows me the new toy. It's just big enough to fit in his hand and he turns it on, gleefully explaining there are twelve speeds. He immediately switches it up several notches and when he touches it to my clit the effect is immediate and energizing.

I'm only able to move my hips a little but soon they're gyrating and swiveling as waves of heat roll through me until suddenly it stops. I whine and whimper and moan and the men laugh at my antics.

Antal wields the stimulator while Grigor plays with my breasts, flicking at my nipples with his tongue. Antal slips his free hand behind me to slide a finger in my anus. He gestures that my hole is unattended and Grigor starts fucking me with his fingers.

"Tits and ass and cunt," says Antal, proud of his English. Grigor repeats the words and the two of them grin at each other. I almost cum while they're distracted by self-congratulation but Antal knows my body too well and he eases up right at the worst possible moment.

After edging me at least half-a-dozen times the men decide I can have the pleasure of sucking dick. The two men flip me onto my knees and kneel at my face, holding their cocks ready. Antal lets Grigor work the sex toy since he has a longer reach and they take turns sticking their dicks in my mouth.

At one point they both try to get inside at the same time and my skinny lips are stretched painfully wide trying to accommodate. They keep fucking my mouth until tears and saliva streams down my face and I'm keening from the brink of orgasm.

Passing instructions in their own language they simultaneously fist their dicks and shoot cum over my face, throat, and chest. It's hot and sticky and I cry out that I want it in my pussy.

Flipping me over again Antal frees me from the sling and they each take an arm and a leg and hold me down while they smear their cum over my skin and stroke everywhere except my nipples and my clit. I know struggling against their great strength is useless but I can't control myself. I'm aching and begging and pleading so I squirm and try to lift my hips.

Finally Antal enters me with one quick thrust and pumps twice before pulling out to make room for Grigor. Same as with their dicks in my mouth they're now taking turns fucking me with just a couple of strokes each. It's very, very hot and I'm ready to explode when, again, they stop.

By now my poor sensitive clit is so blood-engorged that I'm sure I could cum by sneezing. Antal ties me spreadeagled to the bed so I can't use my hands or squeeze my thighs to find relief.

Grigor fetches drinks and cigars and Antal sits in a chair at the foot of the bed to sip and smoke at his leisure while watching me. The two of them pass remarks about my body and my arousal and agree that this punishment is very effective.

I recall that all of this is about punishing me and call out "I'm sorry! I'll be good, I won't be naughty, whatever I did I'm sorry for it and won't do it again. Please, please fuck me, please I'm hurting for you."

Antal approaches with his cigar and draws the unlit end along my slit to wet it before putting it back in his mouth. I watch as he puffs and nods approval at the improved taste. I groan with longing.

I know it will take him about 45 minutes to finish his smoke and thinking this makes me throw a tantrum that really is laughable considering my restraints. All I manage to do is shake like I'm having a fit and both men are highly entertained.

Soon I start to cry in earnest and after about five solid minutes of sobbing Antal gestures to Grigor to fuck me. The big man strokes my cheek telling me that these are good tears, giving me release, it's what he expects when he spanks the naughty she-wolves.

I climax the moment he pushes in deep enough to brush against my clit. Grigor takes his passion and his pleasure seriously, always giving a worthy performance in the bedroom. But he isn't Antal so while the physical act is exceptional... it's specifically Antal's loving that I long for.

Grigor finishes by kissing me on each tear-stained cheek before leaving us alone. Antal keeps me tied down and continues smoking his cigar while observing me. Our eyes hold in a lengthy gaze.

"What did I do wrong, Antal? Why am I being punished?" I finally ask, breaking the silent connection.

"For my pleasure, of course. Tó, you are my favorite toy to play with and now that you've been well-primed and then briefly relieved by Grigor, just think of the powerful orgasms I'm about to give you."

He stands and strips out of his clothes to show off his beautifully inked and muscled body. I'm salivating when he promises: "I'm going to make you howl *kis farkas (little wolf)*."

And he does make me howl until my cries are echoing throughout the house. I pass out from the intensity.

On a few occasions Antal invites his friends to bring in women – hookers, I suspect – and we watch their orgies which can get quite passionately violent. There's always a higher number of men so each woman services several, often at the same time as all their holes get used. The women receive slaps and spanks, get half-strangled, and have their hair pulled. That's the mild stuff, they quickly move on to having a man's cock in at least two if not all three holes at the same time but no one ever complains, in fact everyone seems to revel in their orgies.

One time the men ganged up on another guy and held him down to be buggered. I didn't like to see him struggle but after spotting the smile on Antal's face I kept my thoughts to myself. Grigor applauded so hopefully it was case of them being aware of his latent desires and knowing it was a false protest.

The man was the biggest of them all so he probably could have fought them off but instead he quickly ejaculated during the sex. With a dick still in his ass he got hard again and had the pleasure of a blow job from two women.

Both Antal and I get really turned on watching the naked bodies giving each other pleasure and pain. I sit on his lap and squirm wetly up and down his hard cock until he gives in and fucks me. We never join in with the others, and Antal never hosts an orgy during one of my heats.

He's also bought me clothes. He sat me on his lap while we explored a high-end boutique on an iPad. He picked out dresses and if I nodded he added them to the shopping cart. He vetoed pants or shorts and just laughed when I tried to select some underwear. Obviously he still wants my pussy always bare and accessible.

The dresses he chose are beautiful. Soft, silky fabrics with knee-length skirts that flare and flutter. So feminine! Especially when matched with the several pairs of high-heeled sandals in a variety of colors to complete each outfit.

The new clothes arrived with luggage because he's taking me to Hungary. I've never even been out of the state before, never mind traveling to another country, another continent. I wasn't involved in how he managed the paperwork but sure enough I now possess a passport with a new identity.

We won't be staying with Antal's family, he's the black sheep – if one can say that about wolves! - but we're going to visit Sandor and I will finally be introduced to a large, established pack. Janos is expected to visit at the same time and, of course, Kartal will be there.

The Alphas need to discuss their mutual business and mutual threat. The Fehers haven't let up sabotaging their various operations.

I've been reading a Hungarian to English dictionary and Antal is taking our language classes seriously. We both want to be fluent for each other.

I'm sitting in the garden reading the dictionary downloaded to my Kindle. The sun is warm on my hair so I tilt my head back, eyes closed, to savor the feel of it on my face. That's when the assassins sneak into the garden to capture me.

2

I regret the loss of my new dress when I hear it rip, not from the rough grabbing of me by my would-be kidnappers, but because my muscles stretch and tear the seams when I shift to wolf form.

These attackers have come prepared for a she-wolf with a muzzle and a metal cage but they weren't prepared for my strength. I understand how my slender human shape can mislead them into dismissing me as thin and weak, but as a wolf I'm wiry, sinuous, and strong. Hard to hold onto, vicious when snapping, feral when biting.

The abductors do manage to secure me at last but it took longer than they'd reckoned on which gives Antal and his men sufficient time to come to my rescue. In wolf form they slink into the yard, their entry hidden by the shadows of the surrounding woods and take the intruders completely by surprise.

Thank God the security and surveillance system was recently overhauled so they could get to me in time.

My protectors strike hard and fast because even the deadliest wolf can't fight a bullet. They have to take the men out before they can shoot but did manage to keep one alive long enough to question. He claimed he was just a hired gun who couldn't confirm whether or not his crew was hired by the Fehers, and he died without changing his story.

I hate the cage and howl to be released. Thank fuck Antal warned his men to be vigilant and ready to take action once the watchers became the aggressors.

Grigor shifts back so he can unlock my cage but Antal and I celebrate our victory in wolf form which allows us both to expend the violent energy that's still twanging through us. Me being at risk and in danger makes Antal rage. My hair stands on end as I growl and yip while he bites the ruff of my neck and mounts me from behind.

We were just waiting for my pending heat to come and go before traveling but all this blood and excitement has brought it on now. The sweet scent of my slick sends Antal into rut and he takes me over and over again while nipping me all over. I shift and for a minute or two lie under him, a naked girl, while he marks me with his claws and his slavering jaws huff out hot breaths. It's so frightening and exciting all at the same time. He loves how delicate and fragile my girl's body is lying beneath his wolf.

He shifts before his scratches and bites draw too much blood and we have sex as humans. Of course I still need more so Grigor joins us. I fuck him with wild abandon, the smell of the men who tried to kill me ripe in the air. Grigor moves me into several different positions and when he's exhausted himself Antal is ready again.

I will spend this heat in the company of my Alpha and our Beta. They will protect me and nurture me, insisting I stay hydrated, watching over me when I collapse into semi-conscious sleep, and fucking me constantly. It's a new and wonderfully comforting situation to be guarded by my men.

Antal will send Grigor to fetch the chauffeur who serviced me on the original drive here. They like watching how controlled he is no matter how frantically I wriggle and writhe on his cock begging him to come. At his age he can't fuck repeatedly but he does have the stamina to last and last and last for two times. I think they take bets and time him.

When their dicks get tired we'll play with my toys to keep my pussy fully engaged and get us all through this heat. Then we'll fly to Europe to join up with Sandor and Janos to devise a plot that will end the Feher threat.

I don't feel any trauma from my near-capture, instead I'm angry. Angry that some strangers think they have the right to just pull me away from the best life I've ever had.

This is my home that they invaded. My life that they threatened. My Antal they tried to separate me from... and now this is my fight, too.

3

We fly in a private jet. I've hardly ever been in cars never mind other modes of transportation so it's a new experience for me. And it's terrifying. I'm frightened at how small the jet is, and get scared again during take-off. But when we hit turbulence I totally lose it.

Surprisingly Antal is patient with me. Instead of the smack I expect I get cuddled on his lap. I curl up into a tight ball, as small as I can make myself, and I press hard against his chest. His heartbeat is steady which soothes me, mine is racing a mile a minute.

He rocks me while humming and gradually my breathing calms and my tears subside. I don't have a phobia or a panic attack, just a perfectly rational fear that the plane is going to suddenly stop flying and crash to earth. Except we're over the ocean so I guess instead of burning up in a ball of fire I'll drown.

I'm pretty sure I can swim in wolf form but I've never had the opportunity to find out. Regardless I doubt if I can manage my first swim and fight off sharks at the same time. Predators know their fellow predators weaknesses.

Having a vivid imagination can be a real shit-storm sometimes.

The trip takes quite a few hours and we're traveling at night in order to sleep through most of the journey. As if. I mean, how can we safely fly if I'm not concentrating with everything I've got on keeping the plane airborne?

Antal does drift off but I remain in his embrace and keep kissing all of his skin that I can reach. The warmth of his flesh helps settle me a little bit. I start thinking ahead to the landing and that makes me fret all over again.

When my restlessness penetrates his sleep Antal growls at me for waking him. I start gabbling in a panicky voice which he silences by kissing me. Even my fear of a crash landing can't diminish the sheer Alpha power I feel in his kiss. I'm utterly subdued and seduced, comforted and compliant.

When he breaks off to give me a stern look I start hyperventilating so he kisses me again. I'm fine so long as we're lip-locked, and Antal decides it's a good opportunity to have sex. He pulls my long skirt up, of course I'm naked underneath it, and it only takes him a couple of strokes to get me wet and ready for him.

He unzips and my hot little hands eagerly pull out his cock. I squeeze tightly until he starts leaking pre-cum, then I cup his balls while feeding the head inside me. While I slide up and down he lightly scratches my legs from knee to thigh with his fingernails. His touch is almost as distracting as the pleasurable sensation of being filled to completion. I clench the walls of my pussy around him until I feel him pulsing.

Soon he has one hand holding my ass and the other on my hip while he moves me up and down, faster and faster. I make my pelvis swivel and his cock hits me in all the right places. I cum with a loud cry and he follows a moment later, trying not to vocalize but still a loud grunt escapes him.

I realize then that the pilot and co-pilot can hear us which doesn't bother me unless they stop concentrating on flying the plane. But what if they heard me all fearful and crying about flying? That thought embarrasses me and I force myself to stay calm and still in Antal's arms for the rest of the flight.

He dozes off again but I remain vigilant and quietly alert.

One of the men comes into the cabin and speaks with Antal. He nods in understanding and the man returns to the cockpit. Antal then lifts me off his lap and I tidy us up as best I can. Our fluids have dried but we're sticky. He puts me into my own seat and fastens my seatbelt for me.

I dealt with the arrangements when we came to the airfield at home since everyone spoke English, but now that we're in Hungary Antal will have to take charge.

I don't want him to feel ashamed of me so I force myself to be brave. Although I do grip the arm-rests tightly, squeeze my eyes shut, and have to tell myself repeatedly no crying, no crying!

The actual landing is merely a bump and then we're racing down the runway while the engines whine and gradually slow to a stop. We're safe! Antal's arm comes over my shoulder and he hugs me hard, praising me for being his good girl.

Now I just have to put the idea of our return flight to the very back of my mind.

4

Csilla, Sandor's fated mate, is about Antal's age which is quite a bit younger than Sandor but still about a dozen years older than Tó. She greets them with friendly and warm hospitality, and Sandor stands beaming beside her.

Tó surreptitiously watches Antal to see if he's attracted to Csilla since she's the kind of poised, beautiful, full-figured woman he admires.

They sit down to a light meal that Csilla has prepared for them but Tó isn't hungry. She's actually feeling a bit light-headed. Without even glancing at Tó Antal slips his hand under the table, creeps up under her dress, and plunges a finger into her vagina. While that digit probes for her G-spot his thumb twiddles against her clit. Tó is forced to maintain her composure while listening to the conversation and doing her best to understand the Hungarian. Csilla is bilingual and pauses to translate but mostly the talk is about people Tó doesn't know anyhow.

Kartal enters the room and coming up from behind can see Antal's arm moving and each of Tó's ankles hooked around a chair leg while her bottom flexes. He greets Antal and Tó with a bow and a grin that he doesn't bother to conceal. Sandor catches the look and his gaze moves speculatively to his guests.

Tó makes a point of bumping against Antal's wineglass, grabbing it in time, and saying *bocsánat (sorry)*. She's apologizing for her jealous insecurity, not her clumsiness, which he understands and accepts after delivering a sharp pinch to her clit. She turns her gasp into a cough and he takes the opportunity to smack between her shoulder blades. She knows she can count on getting two disciplinary spanks when they're alone.

That will whet Antal's appetite for punishing sex which means no foreplay. No problem, she's already wet from his teasing. Thinking about him using her that way just ramps up the excitement level. Tó finds his occasional brutality and rough treatment arousing, and will sometimes provoke this reaction with extreme submission. It always works, it's their lupine natures.

After the meal Csilla recommends that Tó and Antal have a rest after their journey, and try to catch an hour's sleep or so. She leads them up a long flight of stairs to their suite. The Koczinyi's live in a real castle although it's a small one. They've spent a fortune to make it comfortable with modern heating, plumbing and electrical.

"Whenever you're ready come back down here and we'll eat cake and drink coffee and get to know each other."

Csilla leaves them and Tó turns to Antal saying: "She's really nice." He narrows his eyes at her and she sighs, knowing what comes next. Sure enough, two sharp spanks accompanied by *no jealousy,* and then being pushed down on the bed with Antal entering her immediately. Tó's snarl is trumped by Antal's growl and the two have sex like they hate each other. Yet when they do finish and fall asleep Tó is wound around his body and Antal holds her tight.

About two hours later they waken, refreshed, and head downstairs. Csilla and Kartal are drinking coffee but Sandor is having a whiskey. Antal joins him in a drink while Tó settles for a piece of cake.

"You look rested," comments Csilla, "Did you sleep well?"

"Like somebody shot a bullet into my brain," replies Tó.

There's a momentary silence after this remark then Csilla turns to Antal saying: "I can see the attraction," and everyone laughs.

After visiting for awhile Csilla offers Tó a tour of her home. They peek into the nursery on the top floor to look at the sleeping children and Tó notices a guard as well as a nanny. She figures that's because of the time a bomb was set off at the children's school but doesn't comment. However Csilla mentions the attack herself.

Then, in a trembling voice, she explains that early tomorrow morning the children will be taken to the family's summer estate in the countryside for their safety. With a heavy sigh she leads the way to her sitting room.

The white-painted wicker furniture is upholstered in shades of peach and a cool blue which gives the room a light, airy feeling that's so different from the rest of the castle with its gray stone walls hung with heavy tapestries.

"I love this room!" Tó exclaims, looking around with delight. "It's so pretty and light and refreshing."

Csilla smiles at the young girl's enthusiasm. Tó isn't at all what she imagined. In her mind she had pictured a brash, confident, and beautiful American girl, not this shy, willowy nymph.

She is so different from Antal's ex-fiancee...

Without understanding why Csilla feels compelled to tell Tó about Beata to give her some insights into her Alpha.

"Antal was born and raised in the next county so Sandor has known him all his life. He comes from a family of Alphas, and while sometimes that can be a good thing, among the brothers in his pack it caused difficulties. Too much aggressive competition between siblings all vying for their father's attention.

The boys were constantly fighting everyone they encountered and, as of result of complaints, they all had to be home-schooled. The jealousy and resentment they felt for each other made their teenage years a nightmare.

Once they matured almost no female was safe. But plenty were willing – all of Antal's brothers are handsome men – however there was talk about everything from inappropriate talk, bad behavior, and even rape.

Antal fell in love with a beauty called Beata, a human who came from an impoverished but well-connected family. They planned to marry but unfortunately Kada, Antal's oldest brother, decided he wanted Beata for himself and, since he's the heir, her family chose him as the better match.

"So Antal had both his heart and his trust broken by the people closest to him."

"Yes, I'm afraid that's true. It made him cold and bitter and... well, vicious and cruel. So when Beata was beaten and brutally assaulted sexually – just before the wedding – Antal was blamed for the crime. He denied it, and since Beata was unable to put a name her assailant no charges were laid. But Kada had Antal banished from the pack."

"What do you think happened?"

"I wasn't here then but Sandor confided that he believed Kada committed the crime against his bride-to-be in order to get rid of Antal. I remember being shocked at the idea and saying surely not but Sandor said he never thought Kada loved Beata, he just wanted to take her away from Antal. And since she was his betrothed he would consider the sex his by right."

"But not the rape, surely?"

"I find him to be a peculiar man, in fact both of them are very odd, in my opinion."

"But Kada and Beata did marry?"

"Oh yes, it was a good alliance on both sides. But they don't have any children."

"Does that mean Antal is currently the heir?"

"No, that would be Gyuri, he's the second son. He's a good friend and we see a lot of him. He has several boys and his wife is expecting again."

"So Antal is probably free of any future family obligation, of being the pack Alpha I mean."

"Yes, probably. Do you think he minds? Does he talk about home and his pack?"

"Hmm, let's just say he doesn't miss them. Tell me, is Beata dark-haired, dark-eyed, very curvy, and big busted?"

"Ha, you've described her perfectly. Oh, does Antal have a photo of her?"

"Not that I'm aware of, but he has shown a preference for a certain type."

"But Tó, Antal is very attentive to you and I noticed that he watches you constantly. You look nothing like Beata but he behaves as if you are his true mate."

Tó smiles shyly at the compliment saying: "I think I feel that way about him, but I grew up as a human, in an orphanage, and I know nothing about packs and very little about wolf-shifters. I've heard of fated mates but..."

"Oh I had no idea, Tó! I'll be happy to answer any questions you have. Let's see, although some shifters will tell you the concept of fated mates is a myth it's not, it's a real thing. I know, because Sandor is my fated mate."

"But wasn't he mated before?"

"He was, but it was an arranged marriage. In fact it was just one of several between two families to join their packs together. Doing one's duty, even making personal sacrifices, for the pack is another very real thing. The health and welfare of the pack is the priority of the Alphas."

"So if a pack rejects a member it's a really serious offence..."

"Banishment is, but I can't think of a single circumstance where a child would be rejected. Did your mother take you and run away? Do you know anything about what happened?"

"I was an infant, left outside a fire station, and there was nothing with my clothes to indicate why I'd been abandoned, just a note saying *Her name is Lake.*"

"Oh that's so sad," Csilla gives Tó a quick hug.

"I guess, but I'm not one to dwell on the past because... well, what's the point? The future is pfft who knows? But I'm pretty good at bitching about the present!" Tó says with a laugh.

Csilla joins in then continues: "But I'm glad you've found happiness with Antal."

Tó wisely keeps her true thoughts about their match made in Hell to herself.

"We're having a few close friends for dinner tonight to meet you and get reacquainted with Antal. My husband thinks we must all acknowledge that the situation with these Fehers is dire. We need to be ready to defend ourselves. I know Janos wants us to be more aggressive but as the mother of small children I'm not anxious to rush into a syndicate war."

"Will this be a formal get-together? Because I don't think I have suitable clothes for that–"

"No worries my dear, my maid will outfit you. She's a style genius and believe me you won't recognize yourself by time she's done!"

A couple of hours later, while staring in the mirror, Tó thinks Csilla's words were prophetic. She truly does not recognize the creature reflected back who wears a sleeveless gown of shimmering ivory satin elegance. Her long platinum hair is freed from its usual braid to be loosely gathered up and secured with a single diamond clip to the crown of her head.

She looks glacial, sophisticated, and regal. The hairclip and a diamond choker sparkle but otherwise her only color comes from her brilliant aquamarine eyes. Csilla raves over her maid's handiwork and says all the staff are exclaiming at how queenly the little American looks now.

When Antal returns to their rooms, immaculately groomed as ever, he studies Tó and his eyes narrow. A flare of his nostrils tells her he's either enraged or overwhelmed by lust – or possibly both. Tó returns his gaze steadily, hiding her trepidation and hoping the rapid pulse in her throat isn't too obvious. That hope fades when his eyes drift to the exact spot and his lips quirk into a tiny smirk.

"Tó, *olyan szép vagy (you are so beautiful),*" says Antal.

Nervously she replies: "*Kösz (thanks).*"

He takes hold of her upper arm much tighter than necessary as her escort. Tó interprets this as possessiveness and discovers she enjoys the feeling. She's also held closely enough to detect whenever Antal stiffens or relaxes, and his minute reactions cue her as they meet the guests gathered in the lounge for pre-dinner drinks. Csilla's *a few close friends* has turned into a party of more than two dozen guests.

As the stranger, the American, Tó expects to be singled out for speculation and whispered comments. What is unexpected is the admiration she sees in the eyes of many. *What a difference haute couture makes*, she thinks to herself.

The simplicity of the gown allows Tó to move freely and she gains a natural poise once the stiffness of the unfamiliar wears off. Being on Antal's arm means she must hold her head high and be a credit to him. The two of them make a stunning picture.

Antal's attention is captured by a dark, slender man who crushes him in a bear hug. Tó has to take a couple of steps back to avoid getting knocked down by the rocking embrace. The stranger speaks rapid Hungarian in an excited, exuberant voice. He kisses Antal on both cheeks and then on his mouth. A passionate kiss that lingers until Antal pulls back. He seems disconcerted but obviously knows the man, smiling and replying to him.

Antal turns to bring Tó forward for an introduction and when she sees the man face on her mouth drops open, she even quietly gasps. This dark-haired man, Stefan, is breathtakingly handsome and Tó can't help but stare. His greeting to her is less than enthusiastic, in fact he's quite formal. He doesn't show her any warmth, and it's obvious he'd be much happier to have Antal all to himself. However Antal pulls Tó away from Stefan after only another minute's conversation.

"Stefan's an old friend, and he's been giving me news of another old friend, Imre," says Antal.

I'm not about to question him in public but once we're alone I'll definitely be asking him about that kiss, Tó decides.

They are separated during the meal, but Csilla has seated Kartal beside Tó so she's able to converse in English and to practice her Hungarian on him. Every time she looks in Antal's direction he's staring at her. But then she realizes she's looking at him just as often. He doesn't return her smile.

People shift a few seats during dessert and Tó is briefly alone while Antal has moved beside Csilla. The two have their heads together in an intimate conversation and Tó feels a twinge of jealousy. She takes a big gulp of the overly sweet wine served with this course and has to fight a gag response. She smooths out her expression to hide her envy and finally turns her head away, determined not to catch his eye again.

Not long after that Csilla draws Tó along with her to the powder rooms to freshen up.

"Tó, Antal has put me on the spot," claims Csilla with a slightly distressed look on her face. "He wants me to pass on a message because he doesn't know the English but, frankly, I'm embarrassed to say the words."

Tó regards her hostess with a grin and motions for her to go ahead. Csilla, as a wife and mother living in a more repressive society, is obviously feeling awkward so Tó suspects the conversation is about to get highly sexual in nature. She's right, but not quite the way she imagines.

"It's best if I just say it quickly and please forgive me in advance for the words and my blushes." Csilla then relays Antal's message in a rush, barely pausing for breath.

"I quote: *you look like such a high-class beauty tonight but that's not the real you since the truth is you are simply my [Antal's] slutty whore. You will be made to strip and crawl naked, begging and pleading, for the punishment appropriate to who you are. Your bottom will be spanked, your breasts will be spanked, and your vagina will be spanked until all of your womanly parts are red and swollen and sore. Then you will suffer the feel of rough hands, rough mouth, rough penis ravishing you till you have no tears left–*"

"Those aren't the words he actually used, are they?"

"No, forgive me but every word he spoke was obscene so I... I'm so sorry, Tó."

"Don't upset yourself Csilla. We both know Antal is a little bit insane but rest assured that those same nasty body parts of his can work magic so his need to abase me is simply part of the price I pay for my pleasure."

When Csilla gives her a doubtful look Tó assures the woman everything she's saying is true and it's all alright.

"Well, if you're sure. And maybe you can explain something for me about English. You just spoke of Antal's need to abase you and I'm sure your usage is correct but why is it abase and not debase?"

"Just so you know, I'm not well-educated in the school sense but I read an awful lot so that's how I've picked up my learning. To the best of my knowledge abase is used when referring to people and debase is used for things. As in debasing the value of something."

"Oh I see. English is a bit of an odd language, and it's not easy to learn."

"Believe me, I'm so glad I was born with English as my native tongue! I think you speak it very well."

"Thank you, and your Hungarian is coming along, too."

Not long after that conversation Antal indicates it's time for the two of them to retire. He impatiently goes through the motion of saying good nights and thank yous with minimal politeness. It's obvious to everyone that he's in a hurry to get Tó alone and she's equally sure they'd be appalled at what he plans to do with her.

She sighs, just thinking about it, and he smirks when he hears. Antal enjoys having her fear what he's going to do, but Tó's concern is *how crazy am I that the humiliation will really turn me on?*

Hurrying her up stairs and down corridors to their rooms Antal practically pushes Tó through the door. He orders her to start crawling.

"I'm willing, of course," she says, "but I don't want to ruin my borrowed gown." She quickly slips out of it and he starts to complain until he catches sight of her.

Did Tó suspect the night would end up this way? No one can know for sure, but she is certainly prepared for it. She's now naked except for high-heels, a lacy garter belt and sheer silvery stockings. Antal circles Tó, his eyes covering every exposed inch, and when she drops to her hands and knees and begin slinking like a panther he growls.

She keeps her head held high and he takes advantage by wrapping his tie around her slender throat. He handles it like a leash and guides her around the room forcing Tó to scramble to keep up. Finally he settles in a chair and commands her to *sit*. She assumes the seated submissive position but doesn't cast her eyes down. Tó keeps up that high-and-mighty attitude which Antal is finding such an enticing challenge.

He instructs her to take off his shoes and socks to massage his feet. When she does this he then orders her to lick the soles of his feet. She complies without hesitation, and bending right down she drags her tongue from his heel to his big toe. Then she wraps her lips around his toe and sucks hard. His expression shows that he's torn between hating her disobedience but loving the sensations. He decides to enjoy the licking and sucking for a bit before pushing her over with his foot.

From her prone position he tells her to spread her legs and show him her cunt. She does so but props herself up on her forearms so she can watch him looking. Any idea that Tó has been holding her own vanish once Antal starts stroking her wet folds with his toes.

He presses down hard on her clit and she spasms. Her face grows hot and she's obviously wondering why it feels fine when he uses his fingers but shameful to cum over his big toe. His detached – almost disinterested – probing at her with his feet feels decadent and dirty. It makes her cry out loudly when she cums.

Antal then instructs Tó to clean the wet mess from his foot so they can repeat the process with his other foot. He knows she's soaked before he even touches her with his toes. He calls Tó his *needy, greedy slut* and she can only nod her head and agree. She'll agree to anything so long as he releases the painful pressure that's built up.

Her mind briefly goes back to the conversation she had with Antal about what it was like to be in heat. Tó explained to him that when she's in that state she simply exists physically, not mentally, and has no shame afterwards over how she might have acted.

It's a totally different thing to this, Tó thinks to herself. *Now I'm aware of what's happening and how it's making me feel. My head and my body are at war with each other. My mind wants him to stop making me blush with shameful desperation, but my pussy is begging and pleading to be carried away on waves of ecstasy. I understand exactly why it's called mindless pleasure.*

I've dripped so much the tile floor is marked with a damp spot.

"Naughty puppy!" exclaims Antal, standing and pushing her nose into the wet spot. The same way a bad dog is trained when it urinates indoors. Having her in this position draws his attention to her ass and thighs so he unbuckles his belt and lays down stripes of pain across that pale flesh.

When she's red enough to please him he flips her over and grabbing both ankles lifts her legs up before pressing them down against her torso. Now the mound of Tó's vagina gets Antal's attention as he slaps it repeatedly with his belt. Her skin must be aching as it heats up but he keeps punishing this sensitive spot despite her writhing and crying. Antal senses when the pain morphs into arousal, powerful arousal, and then he covers Tó with his mouth.

Tó is surprised at her reaction thinking: *I feel the exhilaration more than I feel the hurt.*

He fucks her on the floor. Finishing he stands, still fully dressed, and looks down at the mess she is: her torn stockings, hair falling out of it's clasp, mascara-stained tears streaking down her face, and his tie collaring her neck.

Speaking English slowly but clearly he says: "Mine," and she bites her lip and nods in agreement.

Scooping her up he carries her into the bathroom. The castle doesn't run to shower stalls big enough for two but the bathtubs are delightful. While it fills Antal allows Tó to undress him, then she removes her tattered nylons and garter. He gets in first then lifts her to sit in front of him. Leaning back against his broad chest they both sink into the warm water. He soothes her in his embrace.

That night Antal is woken by Tó's strangled screams, from a nightmare she's having. Waking up, panting from her bad dream, Tó looks around fearfully asking *where am I?*

He holds her close and murmurs reassurance that she is with him and she is safe. He wonders if she's reliving her fear of the plane ride but she says no, it was hearing so much Hungarian being spoken that triggered a bad memory.

It takes Antal some time to coax the details out her. He rubs her arms to warm the goosebumps and get her to relax. Still breathing heavily she relates a story from a few years back when she was an adolescent.

"Puberty was a horrible time for me. Not only was my human body changing but my wolf body, which I didn't even know I had, kept breaking through. I couldn't control my shifting and first I thought I was crazy, then some sort of deviant and then I was afraid I was a werewolf who would go mad, ravaging and killing everyone. There was no one to tell me what was going on. I had to leave the orphanage.

My life there wasn't great but it wasn't terrible either, and I couldn't let this dangerous new other self loose among the younger children. But I had no where to go except the street. As a young teen I was easy prey but I managed to avoid the worst of the humans who attacked me by shifting at least enough to clamp down on a grabby hand with my lupine jaws.

There weren't many places I could go. The homeless shelters always wanted to call Child Services and the library thought I was just a truant. I finally made my home inside a large school. I think it was a college for adults because all the people were grown-ups who were busy and preoccupied and happy to ignore me.

I could go into the library and hide in the stacks. I could nap on sofas in one of the lounges. The labs had people coming in and out at all hours so I could move about freely, too. I often pretended to be one of the cleaning staff."

Throughout this recital Antal listens attentively and doesn't interrupt.

Having set the background of her story Tó explains she would leave the safety of the school to shoplift food, clothes, and toiletries. Sometimes drug dealers would send her on a delivery or a pick-up. She was reliable and always insisted on payment in cash, not product.

One day she was cornered in an alley by a man and a woman. She shifted to escape and was utterly astonished when they shifted too but into foxes. She had no idea such a thing was even possible.

We're much safer then you, little one said the woman explaining that the city-dwellers liked seeing urban foxes and often left out food and fresh water.

This couple helped Tó by teaching her a lot about shifters, and giving good advice on how to get along in the human world. Still, they were foxes and not quite her own kind. Not fully trusting anyone she didn't confide where she lived. So she was heading home on her own at the end of a day spent foraging with the couple when the attack occurred.

"Who attacked you?"

"Wolves. Four or five of them, all males. I knew if I shifted I wouldn't escape unharmed, but if I didn't shift I'd be dead. A she-wolf doesn't stand much of a chance against several males so yeah, I was assaulted and bitten, bitten a lot, but I fought back hard. I had to because at some point in the scrap I realized this wasn't anything sexual – they wanted me dead.

I didn't know much about these wolves and nothing about them as humans. They were connected through a pack and they had specifically targeted me. Finally, luckily, I managed to break free and raced away. I knew where I was going which gave me a slight edge but the males had longer limbs and stronger muscles. I knew I wouldn't have the advantage for long and I don't know if it was my terror or my madness which gave me strength.

One male had stayed close and when he got near enough to tackle me I grabbed hold of his front leg in my jaws and I bit down hard and just kept chewing. He screamed at the others to stop and although he looked the youngest they all listened to him. When I growled and mangled him a bit more he ordered them to leave and when they'd moved back far enough I released him and got away."

"And then? What happened next?"

"Nothing. I avoided that area for about a month and I never saw or heard from them again."

Antal frowns before complaining that he expected more to the story.

"Well... there is one thing but it doesn't make sense which makes me wonder if I heard wrong?"

"What did you hear?"

"It was pretty loud with everyone barking and growling, and it was kind of jumbled so I didn't get the exact words but I had the strongest impression that the wolves had been sent to kill me by... my family."

"To who is your family?"

"I have no idea, that's what's so odd about it. But the wolf whose leg I chewed up? His eyes were the exact same color as mine."

5

When I woke this morning Antal was propped up on one elbow, resting his jaw on his hand, and staring at me. Is it skeevy to watch someone when they're sleeping? I don't feel creeped-out but maybe it is a little psycho-stalkerish... looking deeply into his eyes tells me absolutely nothing. He's the master of no expression.

Fumbling with English and Hungarian I try to ask what he's thinking. I touch his forehead and give him first a quizzical then an encouraging look. That's the extent of my miming ability.

He responds with a gorgeous smile that drives all thoughts out of my head as it melts my heart and ignites my libido. Antal almost never smiles. Humor usually shows as a slight crinkling of the skin below his eyes and the teeniest, tiniest lift at the corner of his mouth. This 1000-watt smile is a steamroller of pure sex appeal that just flattens me.

I know I'm making a ridiculous fool out of myself but he has the strongest magnetic pull and I am utterly helpless to resist him. And dammit he knows it, too.

Antal tenderly brushes my hair back from my face and bending forward places gentle kisses on my forehead, nose, cheeks, and chin. Not my lips although he hovers less than inch away from my mouth. I want to grab his head to pull him close but I also want to remain perfectly still, his doll to play with as he chooses.

His lips finally touch my mouth but with only the lightest pressure. The tip of his tongue licks delicately until I open my lips to admit him inside. It's a soul-searching kiss that's also soul-searing in its tenderness. Who would think that my chauvinist, macho, Alpha can shatter me with sweetness?

Pulling himself up again he slides the duvet down to my waist and moves my hand to my naked breast. I recall how intently he once watched me tease my nipple so I repeat the performance. Trailing my fingers over the small mound of soft breast I circle closer and closer to the hard little bud in the center. From palest pink it darkens as it tightens, even as the small aureole around it puckers and deepens in color too.

My caresses make my breast swell which is noticeable since they're so small. Even though the breath I blow is hot the skin goosebumps and I shiver. Careful not to touch any part of my skin Antal stretches down to lick just the tip of my nipple. The tingling zings through every nerve ending and I involuntarily arch towards him, offering the whole nipple and the whole breast to his mouth.

Instead he tilts my body to expose my left breast and stares at is until I obey his unspoken command. Once again my fingernails are tracing a teasing, arousing path to draw his attention to my aching, needy nipple. Now both swollen breasts are rapidly rising and falling with my panting breaths. Arching and swaying sinuously, my head thrown back and my throat fully exposed, I let my fingers get busy pinching, flicking and twisting both nipples. I'm filled with lust at this edge of pain.

The small close-mouth smile he wears, more of a smirk really, tells me that Antal is enjoying the show. I'm reveling in the hot and cold sensations as I let my body beg for his touch. The girly whispery gasps I give make his gaze intensify and I know I'm close to tempting him out of control.

He pulls the cover right off of me and I press my thighs tightly together to hide my sensitive clit but tightening my muscles only increases the stimulation. I feel the heat of Antal's admiring gaze all over my body, and a flush of desire washes through my pale skin.

"*Olyan szép vagy (you are so beautiful),*" he says. He's said it before but that was the night I was made up like a runway model and dressed in a borrowed gown. This time I translate the compliment with wonder, not caring that I know I'm not beautiful but instead savoring this moment when he insists that I am.

He smoothly turns me over and strokes his hand from the nape of my neck all the way down my back, over my bum, along my thighs, down to my feet which he tickles. I squirm and giggle. With his hands at my ankles he bends down to kiss behind my knees. His nuzzling mouth has found a new tender spot to exploit and I wiggle my hips for him, attracting his attention to my ass.

He bites first one buttock and then the other. Not hard enough to break the skin but I definitely feel the nips and know I'll be wearing his teeth-marks for awhile. I'm easily marred and will enjoy studying the bruises later. He'll ask me if I've checked them out and then he'll want to see the results as well. We both keep a close eye on my body.

He completes his investigation with kisses traveling up my spine and ending with hot licks on my neck and around my ears making me wriggle and moan with pleasure.

When he turns me over he's wrapped both hands around my throat and now I'm struggling to contain my arousal, feeling overcome with want. My legs are splayed in invitation, my nipples are painful points, and my life is pulsing beneath his firm grip. He looks down the length of me and then into my eyes as if searching for my very soul. I'm drowning in desire and he's driven into the depths with me.

He could so easily snap and break my slender neck or tighten his grip to crush my throat and strangle me. It would only take moments and I'm sure he could get the murder covered up here in Hungary.

So it's not just my body that I'm surrendering to him, it's my life. The exchange of trust overwhelms me. He has my whole heart and for the first time I'm struck by the belief that I really do have his. It feels like he loves me... but am I kidding myself? or maybe creating a defense mechanism against a very real peril?

I hope with everything I've got in me that this wordless conversation isn't one-sided. I guess my anxiety shows because suddenly his lips are crashing down on mine, pushing them apart for the invasion of his tongue while he moves between my legs and I guide his hard cock inside my welcoming pussy. We fuck to become one as he penetrates deeply and I absorb every inch. I'm enveloping him in my wet warmth as he fills me.

Afterwards we lie together quietly. I meant to ask him about Beata but, luckily I think, stopped myself in time. I mean, what's the point? Yes, she was an important part of his past but he's not with her now. And what exactly do I want to hear him say? That she's the only one he could ever love? or that she's the most beautiful woman in the world? or *thank fuck I dodged a bullet there?* Yeah, actually I'd like to hear him say that last bit.

It seems likely that what happened was she imprinted on him sexually and broke his heart in the process. Assuming that Antal ever had a heart, that is. But I'm no psychologist.

How could he ever explain in a way I could understand why he's first sexually attracted by; then physically violent with; and finally cruelly indifferent to women who look like Beata. I'm only making the connection because I'd have to be fucking blind not to. Besides, his predilection must be common knowledge if even the enemy, the Fehers, knew to find an assassin to match.

But isn't it possible that instead of punishing Beata for her betrayal of his love the truth is his dark side is what originally drew him to her? I think it's even likely that the first time he saw her his dick got hard and he thought *I'd like to damage that* and then his dick got even harder.

Maybe meeting his inner darkness is why she broke off the engagement? Do I think he's the one who raped and ravaged her? No, because he was quite young then and I think he'd have continued his rampage until he killed her. He has himself under much better control these days but I'm always aware that it's never 100 per cent.

So we lie in each other's arms without conversation. Being here doesn't feel like we're on a vacation but how would I know? I've never had a holiday. We are definitely in a different frame of mind. There's no need to get up, but as guests we should try to disrupt the family's daily routine as little as possible. But this is a castle with servants so perhaps those courtesies aren't expected? Maybe I'm only considering this because I am, or was, a servant myself?

We're in a strange place, well... strange to me. That thought prompts me to ask Antal if things look familiar or has it changed a lot? I don't know how long he's been away from his homeland, his family and pack.

Abruptly he sits up but doesn't get out of bed. Instead he shocks me by scooting down between my legs and spreading them wide. He slides his fingers up my slit, diddles my clit for a moment, then slides them back down. He does this several times and then replaces his fingers with his tongue. His touch is electrifying.

Although Antal demands that I perform oral sex pretty much daily it's a much rarer event for him to go down on me. Too bad, because he's so good at it. When he sucks my clit into his mouth and brushes it with his teeth it's like fireworks have exploded in my pussy. And my head feels like I'm being swept backwards into an arc that lifts my whole body. I'm sure I scream, maybe even howl, in delight.

Then he just stays crouched, staring into my eyes with my cum shiny on his chin, while his fingers get busy again probing inside my hole, searching out my G-spot and pressing his thumb on my clit. It's a familiar caress that shatters me every time. Excitement builds quickly and I know I'm going to cum again but for some reason my eyes fill with tears. I'm used to Antal edging me so what's different now? I'm really struggling to hold all this emotion inside.

When he reaches up to stroke an escaping tear I see his pupils have dilated. He might be aroused thinking I'm crying from pain but I need to explain my reaction. "I'm feeling too much, inside here," I strike my chest to demonstrate. "It makes it hard to breathe. It's too much, too much feeling."

Without warning he plunges deep inside me and starts a frenzied pounding. Each stroke punishes and pleases and I cum hard but he doesn't miss a beat. I'm thrashing along his length and he reacts with a sensuous groan but still he keeps stroking steadily. My fluttering squeezes bring me to the peak again and this time he bites down on my shoulder and joins me in orgasm.

He's broken the skin and that hurt, but it's also dispelled the suffocating loving tenderness that was overwhelming me. He somehow sensed that I needed rescue.

I can't love Antal because I'm incapable of such feeling and he's utterly unloveable. But right now we're clasped in a tight embrace and he's murmuring *jó kislány (good girl)* over and over again and I'm replying with *thank you, my Alpha.*

6

We are visited today by Imre, Antal's childhood friend, but their greeting is restrained. I know Antal left Hungary in a hurry and in disfavor with both his family and the community. I'm not sure if these two maintained their friendship since then. Imre is the man that the gorgeous Stefan mentioned.

Csilla escorts Imre to our rooms but not with her usual warm friendliness. Something's up, and when I see how she keeps Imre under close observation I feel a twinge of alarm.

The men speak their language so rapidly I can't hope to keep up. Imre is enthusiastic while Antal appears to be responding to, rather than initiating, the talk. Imre is a very handsome man, not in the same class as Stefan or even Antal, but good-looking and knows it.

Under the cover of their loud conversation Csilla explains Imre has a bad reputation for having a nasty, vicious streak and encouraging this deviance in Antal. Or vice versa, the local families haven't made up their minds about who is the likeliest offender.

Csilla introduces me since Antal has made no move to do so and Imre gives me his attention with a laser-like focus. He shows his skill by engaging with flattering intensity, but I am not disarmed by his tactics.

A servant comes and whispers to Csilla who looks torn over a decision. Finally she apologizes and excuses herself to deal with the household issue.

I can grasp enough of what the men are saying when Imre gestures to me and asks: *Yours?* And Antal nods once, stating: *Mine.*

Imre speaks quickly and I'm struggling to understand. It seems Imre is suggesting he and Antal re-enact some good times by playing with me. Actually it sounds like he's saying punishing me but that can't be right... oh!

I discover that Imre is fluent in English when he turns to me explaining Antal is being difficult, refusing to let Imre punish me but wavering at the idea of me being disciplined by him. *Is there a difference?* I wonder.

Now it's Antal who is having trouble keeping up with the conversation when I squawk: "What do you mean about disciplining me?"

"Well I won't draw blood... but I will do my best to make you scream."

He actually smiles at me while saying that and it's not the sneering smirk of a TV cartoon's Dastardly Villain, but a grin of pure enjoyment in anticipation. I'm horrified to realize this man is a *bona fide* sadist.

After another rapid-fire exchange in their own language Imre proudly announces that he's convinced Antal to let him have his way.

"I said that letting me play with you – in ways he and I enjoyed playing with many girls in the past – is no different than letting other men fuck you when you're in heat. So let's begin."

Imre comes up to me with an unholy light in his eyes and begins removing my clothes. I turn to Antal who simply watches impassively.

"Antal tells me he never punishes you because you're a very obedient Omega for him. I've assured him that even good submissives need to be disciplined regularly so they understand the consequences of disobedience."

"He punishes me all the time!" I exclaim. "His favorite thing is to edge me." "Ah, but I'm talking about corporal punishment, Omega."

"And he's agreed to this?"

"Yes! But he says just a taste. So I will have to be satisfied with that. I'd much rather thrash you until you're nothing more than a bleeding, sodden puddle on the floor."

I flinch at the hated word *puddle,* the mean nickname bestowed on me by the perfect blondes at the Gentlemens Club back before Antal rescued me, but I can only spare a moment's thought to that because Imre is still talking. All the time he's speaking his seductive baritone strokes me as if promising pleasure yet this man's pleasure is someone else's pain. Agonizing pain. *My* agonizing pain.

I was all set to argue with Antal but instead we lock gazes and I match his usual lack of expression with a stoniness of my own. I stand tall , unashamed of my nudity to show him that I'm strong enough to take whatever he allows this friend from his youth to give.

Now that Imre has finished stripping off my clothes he studies me from every angle while speaking out loud to himself. He's commenting on the whiteness of my skin being the perfect canvas for his strokes, and how my delicate bones, protruding at neck, ribs, and hips, are so fragile and alluring.

"I don't suppose anyone has a nice bamboo cane?" he asks. "I guess I'll have to use my belt but it's thicker then I'd like and.. aha!" looking around the room he's paused at an artful display of weaponry on the wall.

"An epee will do but oh look here, even better yet, a foil. Thinner and whippier with just the flick of a wrist."

He takes down the skinny sword and demonstrates with a whistling slash. Everything inside me grows cold and I'm practically paralyzed with fear. So much for my show of bravado, panicked I turn to Antal crying: "Seriously? a SWORD???"

But it's Imre who answers, scoffing as he explains a foil has no edge, just a sharp pointed end except that this weapon has been capped. He rubs it across his palm to show that it can't cut. But it is still a steel implement, whip-thin.

"Turn to face your Master so he can see your tears," instructs Imre. "And place your hands on your knees."

I'm looking right at Antal as I get into position as ordered. The men exchange a few words and Imre translates that Antal wants me to pull my shoulders back and show him my tits. So much for getting a reprieve. I comply just as Imre continues asking:

"You can see her face, right? And you've noticed her eyes – that color...Haven't you wondered about...?"

Antal just nods, his face closed to further conversation.

Imre runs the foil down my body from neck to ass. He rubs me a few times before delivering a stinging stroke that drives me up on my tiptoes. The pain is instant and severe, I feel like I've been sliced with a knife. My eyes water and I hiss in a sharp breath.

My punisher leaves enough time for me to fully experience the burn before he swings his arm in the opposite direction and now my flesh has ignited with a blistering heat. The pain is immense and I feel the tears spill out of my eyes to stream down my cheeks.

I've held my position but I'm panting as I try to breathe through it, on the verge of shrieking.

I'm aware that Imre is winding up for another hit when Antal shouts *elég! (enough!).*

I straighten up which means Imre catches me on the plumpest part of my bottom when he ignores Antal and follows through with his third swing. This time I jump from the stinging pain but am thankful Imre didn't connect where he'd planned – the extremely sensitive part at the very top of my thighs.

Antal is on Imre with a roar, wrapping his hands around his friend's throat. Imre's lids droop over eyes lit with lust as Antal strangles him. Does Imre see it as an act of erotic asphyxiation? or is he simply in love with Antal? All I know is that the evidence of his body's arousal shows that Imre is mightily turned on by Antal's touch – although assault would be a more accurate word.

Csilla hurries back in gasping *Tó, you're naked!* and *Tó, you're bleeding* at me, and *stop! you're killing him* to Antal. Antal flings Imre away from him and Imre rubs his throat, loudly sucking in air and coughing hoarsely.

I twist to look over my shoulder to see my damaged ass, but before I can Antal turns my backside his way and growls out angry noises that sound like he's cursing.

Reaction has set in and I start a violent trembling. Csilla snatches an afghan off one of the couches to cover and warm me, careful to avoid my welted ass, then pulls me into her soothing, motherly embrace.

Yelling and fighting again breaks out between Antal and Imre who seems indignant over Antal's reaction. Yanking at his arm Antal pushes his erstwhile friend out of the room, and forces him to leave.

Both Csilla and I breathe sighs of relief once he's gone. Antal starts pacing around us, angrily, but I know better than to expect an apology.

He growls and mutters in Hungarian until Csilla releases me. Antal grabs my chin and tilts my face up so he can look in my eyes for a typical wordless study. Bending he lifts me up so I'm lying over his shoulder and I hear Csilla's cry of dismay at the sight of me. The tickling sensation I feel means bloods is flowing freely.

"At least it's red..." She's mumbles the words under her breath but Antal speaks sharply and they have a heated exchange heated in their own language.

Antal heads into our bedroom and gently lays me face down on the soft feather mattress. He gets up beside me, half reclining, as his fingers lightly trace over the three slashes. It's the third stripe having cut through the other two that caused the bleeding which has already stopped. Now there are just tiny red drops welling up to dot the lines.

A moment later Csilla returns to hand something to Antal, then inexplicitly says to me "Don't worry, Tó. Sandor and I decided from the start not to notice anything. Your secret, or whatever is going on, is safe with us." Then she leaves.

Antal opens up the jar she gave him and dabs a soothing lotion over my bruises. Then he lays his head on my lower back and blows a cooling breath over me.

I want to ask him to explain what Csilla meant but his gentleness, combined with his obvious regret, pulls a storm of sobbing from me. He kisses the back of my head and rubs my back in a circular motion that calms me. Then he stretches out and places my tear streaked face against his chest, rocking slightly until I'm lulled to sleep.

Part Four

The Danube travels through a couple of countries en route to Hungary and flows through a few more when it leaves. Many small waterways branch off and Antal takes me to a favorite childhood spot not too far southwest of Pest.

We've borrowed a car and drive by a couple of beaches before arriving at an out-of-the-way spot. It's deserted. The weather has put off the swimmers but high stony banks shelter us from the strong wind. Walking along the water's edge we bask in the warmth of the sun.

Antal carries the heavy picnic basket Csilla had made up for us, and I've got the blanket. Our free hands are linked together. It's a closeness that feels completely alien to our relationship and yet at the same time – completely right. I've never been on a real date, but I imagine this is what it would be like. I suspect any dating Antal has done is far back in his past.

We both take off our footwear to enjoy dipping into the icy cold water. The comforting warmth of his hand in mine, the vivid colors along the banks, the fresh smell carried by the brisk breeze all combine into a heady sensual experience. By time we reach the spot Antal remembers from years ago I'm electrified with arousal.

I give the blanket a vicious flap to spread it out quickly and immediately reach to pull him down beside me. Antal chuckles at my eagerness, but as I draw him close and lock my hot mouth on his he's soon humming with pleasure. He's being surprisingly amenable.

He gives over control to me and I revel in it. Pushing him down on his back I unbutton his shirt and unbuckle his belt. I feel his hard cock but I leave it in his jeans while rubbing the heel of my hand along its length. I know the stiffness of the denim will add to his stimulation. My

146

little hands knead his shoulders while I lay kisses from his throat to his nipples. I gently comb his chest hair through my fingers that then walk their way down his hairline to his navel and beyond.

He's holding his breath when I unzip his fly to pull out his cock. Bending down I fill my mouth, drawing him down my throat, worshiping it. He wraps his hands around my head massaging my scalp as I bob up and down along his shaft. Inhaling deep breaths I move down further and further, mastering my gag reflex, until pubic hair tickles my nose. He's given me almost daily opportunities to perfect my performance and I'm quite proud of my fellatio skills.

I gently cup his balls and feel his body go rigid but before he cums he pulls me up to straddle him, yanking up my dress and ripping my panties aside. Fighting to stay in charge I place my hands on either side of his waist and hold myself up away from his body. Our only point of contact is his dick sliding in my hole. I bend my head to watch my hips moving up and down – exactly the way my mouth did moments before – and the sight of his veiny shiny cock slipping in and out of view is such a turn on.

Antal groans and looking at his face I see that he's watching too. Our eyes meet and I give him a wicked grin before rapidly jackhammering my hips and his shout of delight is enough to drive me over the edge. I squeeze my insides as tight as I can and drag him along with me.

Afterwards I curl against his broad chest and he holds me safe and secure in his muscular embrace. I don't know if it's because we're away from all the friendly but inquisitive eyes at the castle, but here we're able to completely relax. We're lazy and unhurried and comfortably satiated.

We converse in our broken language – a mixture of English, Hungarian and mime. I understand that this was a place he came to as an adolescent when he needed to escape the confinement of living with his family in a large clan. I'm flattered that he's sharing this private spot with me. I suppose Imre came here with him back in the day but neither of us have mentioned Imre and I'm not starting now.

We discover that the picnic basket was heavy because of the alcohol. He tells me we'll save the bottle of *Pálinka* for later, and have wine with our meal. He pours some into glasses while I lay out all the packets of food. We're both hungry and soon eat our way through cheeses, cold meats, and dark rye bread. I drink a couple of glasses of wine, but Antal opens the second bottle and finishes that himself. Now he lies back down and stretches out for a sleep.

I sit up cross-legged looking out at the water for awhile. When I turn back to study his face I notice how calm he looks, the lines around his mouth smoothing out a bit as his muscles relax. I have no idea how old Antal is, but I think probably about fifteen years older than me. His hair is thick but I see a few threads of gray above his ears. I have no memory of my father but regardless I know Antal is certainly no replacement daddy. The thought makes me giggle and I see his eyes moving beneath his lids at the sound. I keep quiet, wanting to let him get his rest.

Sitting here is so peaceful. I still haven't caught sight of a single soul, not even a boat out on the water. Resting my chin on the palm of my hand I stare out at the horizon with no thoughts crowding my head – just enjoyment of the moment. My mind's a million miles away when Antal says my name and I turn to him with a smile.

He pulls me down for a kiss and our garlicky tongues stroke together as he lazily sweeps his through my mouth. We share our breath and as so often happens when he deep kisses me it feels like time is standing still. Eventually we break apart and I ask him what the date is. He pauses to think before answering.

"Oh!" I exclaim, "Yesterday was my birthday. I'm twenty-one now."

He tells me he'll buy me a present and that we'll celebrate at the castle with a cake and everyone will sing. I stare at him in horror. All those people looking at me? What would I do while they sang? No, no, I tell him. We'll just have a private celebration on our own.

No one celebrated birthdays in the orphanage where I grew up although we all knew our birthdates. When we reached our teens the administrator helped us write to the Vital Statistics office to get a copy of our birth certificates so we could get Social Security Numbers.

I never got my birth certificate. I applied, but was forced to leave the home before it arrived. If it ever did, maybe my parents never registered my birth?

After an interlude of snuggling and kissing we pack up and make the long walk back to the car. The sun is setting and without its warmth we feel a real chill in the air. Winter is still a ways off but it's coming.

Antal puts the basket and blanket in the trunk and takes out a long knit cardigan for me and a hoodie for him. He tosses the garments in the back seat since we don't need them in the car. I don't drive, not even in America with an automatic transmission, so I usually don't pay much attention to the route, but it doesn't feel like we're heading back to the city. I can't read the road signs here and nothing looks familiar.

"Where are we going, Antal?"

"To a place to drink Pálinka and see stars," he replies. Or at least that's what I understand him to say.

"Okay, what's Pálinka?" He smiles like I've got a real treat in store explaining it's a famous Hungarian brandy.

We travel a dual highway for about twenty minutes only seeing the occasional vehicle, usually a truck, heading in the other direction. Antal turns off onto a badly graveled road that leads up and up. He has to work the gears to push the car to reach the top.

The moon's light shines out like a cinematographer's wet dream and spotlights a ruin that could believably be Dracula's castle. It's stunning and dramatic and oh-so eerily romantic.

Antal passes me the sweater and a flashlight. He takes the hoodie and the Pálinka. There is an overgrown path that I shine the light on while he takes a swig straight from the bottle. We trade the bottle and flashlight back and forth as we walk, keeping an eye on our feet to avoid the treacherous roots and slippery vines that clog our way.

Entering what remains of the ancient building Antal sits on a waist-high wall and pulls me up into his lap. The dank chill of the air permeates my bones and I'm glad I'm not sitting on the cold stone. Antal doesn't seem to notice but the way he's chugging the Pálinka might have something to do with that! It's a tasty fruit brandy and no doubt packs a real punch. Antal probably shouldn't be driving when we head home but I won't be complaining. It's not like I can drive instead, and I wouldn't dream of telling Antal what to do.

Besides, my observations have led me to believe our wolfish nature gives us more tolerance. I don't know why, it's not like alcohol is part of an animal's regular diet! but maybe it has something to do with our resilience? with our metabolism? who knows?

I am warm enough with his arms wrapped around me and the fruity liquor burning in my belly. Then he tilts my chin until my head falls back and I'm looking up at a billion stars in the black velvet sky. I'm transported out of my body – away from chills and cravings – and am wholly lost in the glorious night view. I tuck my head under Antal's chin and the two of us just stare our eyes full. I've never seen anything like it.

I've heard of light pollution but I've lived my whole life in the city so I have no real concept of its meaning. Or I never did have, until now. The longer I stare the more twinkling lights I can see. And even though the sky is inky black there's noticeable depth and millions and millions of stars. And the moon is full, super bright and so big. It looks really close, too. Everything is stunning.

"Oh Antal," I say. "This is so very beautiful, and so special."

He tightens his hold and answers in his deep, sexy voice: "Beautiful Tó is special. Special to Antal."

Emotion overwhelms me but with warmth, not tears, this time. All I can think is: fuck my life I'm in love with a psycho and maybe he's in love with me, too. That's a scary, thrilling, exciting, unbelieveable, impossible thought but... maybe?

I snuggle closer instead of trying to answer.

After awhile Antal shivers and that wakes me up enough to suggest we head back. I feel sleepy but in case Antal is drunk I have to help him drive – in my head, of course, same as how I kept the airplane aloft – so I force conversation out of him by asking the names of the road and any villages we pass by. I ask about the ruins and he relates what he knows of the history. We manage to stay alert enough to get back to the castle safely and without attracting the attention of the *rendőrség (police)*.

In the early morning hours Antal wakes up to find me holding a pistol to his forehead. I decide the best way to handle being in love with a psycho is to be one myself. He frowns while trying to figure out what the object is... then realizing the truth gives me his most devastating smile. His chest hums with a rumbling purr of pleasurable excitement.

He bought me this gun. It's a *Lady Derringer*, a 45, and it's so cute. I mean it's lethal, but it's tiny and I can hold it easily. There's even a fancy floral design on the grip. This is what he ordered for me at the shooting range. Since we flew on a private jet Antal said I could bring it with me but to keep it concealed during boarding and deplaning.

"You shoot me?" he questions, seductively smiling.

I tilt my head as if considering the idea then I run the tip of my tongue along my teeth and I see interest spark in his eyes. *Noooooo,* I draw the word out. Then I stroke his cheeks with the gun, run it across his lips, and order him to open up. When he does I slide the short barrel into his mouth.

Staring at the picture this presents I realize this is how I look when I'm sucking his cock – except for the very different lengths. I ease the gun back and forth and though it fails to come anywhere near the back of his throat it does rub along his tongue. He makes mmm-mmm noises and I start to giggle.

"Stop that! You're supposed to be terrified of me."

To show me just how unthreatened he actually feels he folds his arms behind his head and damn, there's that panty-melting smile again. It works, even when his lips are wrapped around a gun barrel. Maybe it's even hotter this way? but that might just be weird me.

I take the gun out of his mouth and run it down his chin, throat, chest, belly – pointed to shoot – until I pull the duvet aside and reach his cock. It's as hard as the steel barrel and just as much of a weapon. All the while he's watching me with interest, seeing how turned on I'm getting over this feeling of power. Such a little weapon but deadly.

Stroking the gun up and down his shaft, bouncing his balls with it, and then sliding it to his asshole I ask: "Should I put this inside your hole? or mine?"

The words barely leave my lips before he's disarmed me and reversed our positions so that now he's the one on top sliding the little gun inside my wet pussy. On the verge of orgasm I cry out my warning before I start thrashing around:

"Antal! It's loaded!"

My crash into ecstasy is accompanied by his laughter.

2

When I first met Janos wife and fated mate Erzsébet I was struck by her beauty. This tall, well-built redhead looked me up and down after the introductions and snorted in surprise. I sniffed eagerly at her wonderful woodsy, musky perfume and she enveloped me in a tight hug. I saw Csilla relax with relief and I didn't dare look at Janos. Antal, as usual, didn't react in any way. But each time I see Erzsébet I'm in awe all over again. I can't imagine such a confident beauty being publicly stripped, beaten, and screwed.

After our first meeting Csilla told me that Erzsébet took her aside to say she can't believe she earned herself a punishment for jealousy over such a skinny child.

I'm not a child, I replied. *But, I'm certainly no threat to a beautiful woman like Erzsébet.*

My three Alphas, as I think of them when they're together, have business to discuss and meet each morning for a lengthy session. I've been spending that time with Csilla and Erzsébet and I think the three of us are close to being friends. I've never really had friends before. There was the fox-shifting couple I knew in my early teens, but there's never been anybody else.

I don't have a lot in common with these two women who are both older and Hungarian but I like listening to their conversation. Erzsébet has a little English and Csilla translates the rest. After several days in their company I can tell my Hungarian is getting better. Maybe not so much with the speaking and pronunciation but it's a lot easier to understand what they're saying. The one thing we definitely have in common is that I've had sex with their husbands but that fact will hardly bring us together and it isn't mentioned.

When in the company of the Alphas I've been very careful to avoid eye contact and I never initiate conversations. I've felt Janos' gaze on me but I purposely keep my eyes averted because when he's watching me Erzsébet is watching too.

Sandor told me he was amazed at how I had changed since they were in America. I proudly told him I've gained almost twenty pounds under Antal's care. Csilla had to translate that I meant about 9 kilos, and both she and Erzsébet exclaim that I'm still skinny so how tiny was I back then?

"I was scrawny and always hungry, too. Antal has put me on a diet to gain weight and I'm in trouble if I don't eat." I say the words fondly and looking at him see he's got that tiny smirk slightly lifting one corner of his mouth. No doubt reminiscing about punishments I've received when I've gotten myself into trouble with him.

His expression turns regretful as he tells them that I will never have *nagy cicik (big tits)* and they laugh when I roll my eyes. Taking my hand he raises it to his lips in a courtly gesture that he totally ruins by then shoving it into his groin and squeezing it against his cock. I yank my hand away when he says: "Tó is my *jó kis ringyo (good little slut)*." The men laugh, Erzsébet frowns, and Csilla just shakes her head indulgently.

It's a new experience for me to sit with other people as an equal, or almost one, socializing. I like it. Antal did inform Csilla about my birthday and of course she arranged for a cake. I blushed while receiving everyone's good wishes and toasts and I smiled so hard my cheeks hurt. I think this is what it means to be happy, and Antal was very pleased with himself.

Ever since Csilla mentioned that he's always watching me I've paid attention and it's true. His eyes are almost always on me and if I see him looking elsewhere his gaze soon returns. She's a romantic and thinks he's smitten but I believe it's his innate possessiveness, and his need to own and control me. Sometimes when I catch his eye I wink. Either his lips will give that tiny twitch that passes for a smile or he frowns, depending on his mood.

One afternoon when the men come out of their meeting Janos collects Erzsébet for a trip into the city and Csilla leans in for a private conversation. I'm a little apprehensive when I see that she's nerving herself to speak. Glancing at her husband and seeing that he and Antal are still deep in their conversation she begins.

"Tó, when my husband was in America he told me... well, I knew, actually, that he'd been unfaithful to me. With you. He explained you were in heat and as an Alpha trapped in close proximity with you in that state he couldn't control himself and I... well, um, I just, uh wondered–"

"Oh Csilla. I'm so sorry about what happened. I'm embarrassed to be meeting you now, in your home, but honestly I didn't know and–"

"I'm not blaming you, Tó! No, not at all. I just wondered about Sandor and how he was with you."

"I have no idea. I can't remember and that's normal, for me, I mean... you're an Alpha too, right?"

"I am."

"So I don't think I can explain adequately but when I'm in heat I have no idea what is going on or who is around or what we're doing. My one overriding thought is that it isn't enough, no matter how much I get I want, I need, more. It's like in summertime when it's so hot and humid that the air kind of shimmers and everything looks distorted. Or maybe it's more like fog, where you can't see but you can feel and hear and taste and... because your eyes are blinded every other sense is more attuned. I'm sorry that probably sounds silly."

"No, I get the idea and... wow, Tó it sounds horrible."

"It really is! But I'm young and still new to heats and how to handle them. It's a million times better now that I'm with Antal and have his protection. I was always so frightened when I was on my own. Omegas are always vulnerable but even more so when we're being especially needy and whiny.

To try to answer your question all I can say is I have no bad memories of Sandor and how he treated me. Although to be honest Antal was pretty much the only man I was aware of. I distinctly remember trying to climb him like a tree because I wanted... um, to kiss him? No, that doesn't sound right. Oh I know – I had an overpowering need to see the tattoos at the base of his neck." I start to laugh recalling the sense of urgency I felt, adding, "Then, when I reached my goal and could see into his eyes I backpedaled so quickly!"

Csilla laughs too saying: "I can imagine! Being around Antal can be unnerving enough when you know him never mind when he's a stranger."

The men turn when they hear our laughter. I think Sandor has a slightly sheepish look which is kind of a funny way to describe an Alpha wolf! but whatever he sees in his wife's face reassures him. Antal, on the other hand, simply narrows his eyes in suspicion. Kartal just chuckles and I smile back hoping my expression looks sweet.

3

We've come to Hungary so Antal can meet with family and associates to plan a counter-offensive against the Fehers. They've made damaging forays by snapping at the edges of our circle like coyotes but we're wolves and we attack head-on.

I don't know everything that's going on because I'm still shaky on the language, definitely out of my depth with all the innuendo and shared history between these packs, and unschooled in the ways of a rich people's underworld.

Everyone has a story of an attack to relate. Csilla's was certainly the most frightening because of the children. Even among crime syndicates certain things, like the children of the family, are left untouched. Trouble is, the Fehers consider us shifters as non-human lesser beings so they think different rules apply. They're about to learn that they're wrong.

Again it was mentioned that the bomb could have been intended to harm one of several politician's whose children attend that school. That's the official police view. As we discover during the discussions the possibility exists that each attack could have a second explanation.

When the wheel came off Erzsébet's sports-car after she had her snow tires put on it could have been deliberate malice from a Feher or shoddy work from the garage.

The night all the cars in the nightclub parking lot had slashed tires and knife scoring through the paintwork could have just been garden-variety vandalism.

But when you start to add the incidents together: fires at two warehouses, every window in the lobby of their headquarters smashed, employee emails phished and viruses sent on freebie promotional flash drives... it's hard to come up with a different explanation for the total sum.

In addition, the episodes on American soil argue a personal knowledge, or at least in-depth surveillance, of the victims. The only time Tó is ever alone, ever left unattended, is when she's relaxing with a book in the garden. Even then she usually has company because Antal is a very jealous and possessive man. The drive-by shooters and her would-be abductors must have learned her routine and awaited their opportunity.

But they hadn't expected the wolves to attack so quickly and thoroughly so maybe it wasn't the Fehers behind the attempt? Maybe it was just opportunistic assailants, ransomers, traffickers...? who had no idea the home was occupied by shifters. Antal owns a very big home in a wealthy neighborhood. The distance between houses and the privacy of mature trees means the property is mostly hidden from view.

The woman who came to assassinate Antal was assumed – by everyone, himself included – to have been procured according to his specific tastes. Because she was exactly his type the guards at the door didn't think twice to let her in. It was only a sixth sense or some protective instinct that warned Tó this woman was different. Maybe her jealousy made her especially vigilant. Antal has made enemies of his own, it's a by-product of their business, but the possibility is unlikely.

The other argument in favor of the occurrences being planned attacks rather than unfortunate coincidences is that the Fehers are struggling to build their empire. For some time they have been attempting inroads on the packs' territory believing themselves superior simply because they're human. Disregarding centuries of trusted relationships between the united packs and their clientele.

They are upstart incomers who never stood a chance of taking over but that lesson cost them a lot of money to learn. Now they're desperate, faced with financial ruin, when it's their own deaths they should be fearing more than the loss of money. Apparently the problem is the son of the family, the heir, a rash young man called Mór.

Mór is impatient, demanding, and headstrong. He won't take advice but he will take plenty of risks. His actions are causing a rift among the Feher family and their associates.

Mór is too volatile and too inexperienced but also too arrogant to admit these faults so he's very dangerous. And his forays have met with some success. Enough to cause delays in fulfilling shipments, and transportation slowdowns that negatively impact the syndicate's reputation for reliability.

The planning and plotting of coordinated attacks to squash the Fehers has heated everyone's blood. Minor feuds between the packs are put aside while every effort is concentrated on what Sandor calls a surgical strike.

Antal's vicious streak is stoked and after every meeting we have a violent sexual encounter. It's painful – for me – but always thrilling for both of us. Raw passion fueled by the dark desires of vengeance, ruthlessness, and bloodlust. Each of us is rough with the other, blessedly free of confusing emotionalism, but still I suffer the brunt of his anger.

I can see Antal's rage grow like a living thing when he relates the story of my almost-abduction. He is simmering like a pot on the boil when we return to our rooms. I feel a frisson of real fear but know that there is no diverting him from whatever he has in mind for me. I simply have to get through it. I am fully aware of the irony that fear for my safety causes him to imperil it.

I obey his order to strip and I'm sure the looks I cast his way are full of trepidation but his face remains impassive. Positioning me on the bed he ties my wrists and strings me up to the top rail of the tester. I'm kneeling, but barely touching the surface of the bed so my wrists are bearing a lot of my weight.

Yanking open the drawer of the bedside table Antal extracts a flogger. He's swishes it down on the bed a few times so I can get a good look at it. It's leather and made up of many thin strips with a long, thick handle to allow a full-motion swing of his arm that will end in a thud.

Floggers can be used to teasingly tickle or viciously punish. The best I can hope for is something slightly to the nasty side of center.

He tosses it down on the bed and turns back to search in the drawer again. This time he pulls out a double-flogging device. This is a length of thick metal chain attached to two floggers which have finger loops instead of a handle. Antal slides both his left and right hands into position then starts rotating his wrists so the strips fly like propellers. The short chain serves to keep the floggers in place for more controlled hits.

The whirling whips bite into my skin with sharp stings and I try to arch my body away. It isn't agonizing, actually it's arousing, yet still painful. The hits don't break my skin, but I feel my flesh grow hot as is reddens from the burn. I writhe and twist in a futile effort to escape but also to squeeze my thighs together trying to capture and rub my clit. I can't help myself. Antal is determined to deliver a lengthy punishment which I'm sure will bring me to climax. The beating is pleasurably, painfully stimulating. I drift into the head space that has guarded me from my reality for my whole life.

I view Antal with detachment. I can see his reflection, along with my own, in the large mirror on the opposite wall. He's twirling his wrists like he's wielding nunchucks and wearing a look of angry concentration. His scowling expression still can't hide his masculine beauty. Focusing on that is a good distraction from what my body is suffering. My own face is screwed up with open-mouthed crying. Nevertheless I see that my squirming has a sinuous quality, and my nipples are hard and red.

Sometimes the tips of the floggers catch my back but most are slashed down on my behind and thighs with his left-handed right-handed strokes. I can see how my naked body undulates with each strike, but I wish I could watch how he makes my bottom dance because apparently he's entranced by the sight.

Evidently the double-flogger is sufficient to satisfy his purpose. He tosses it to the floor and to my great relief doesn't pick up the larger implement. I've reached the point where my need for sexual satiation, not more punishment, is overpowering.

Antal grabs my sore ass and starts gently squeezing and rubbing which soothes some of the sting. He rests his chin on my shoulder so we're both looking at ourselves in the mirror.

Placing one knee between my legs he lifts me enough to ease the pressure on my wrists and I'm grateful for that mercy, but then we both notice how this position exposes my slick folds and red clit. While one hand continues to palm my hot butt the other slips round to torment my vulnerable bud which he barely touches before I explode in orgasm.

My body has learned to derive pleasure from the pain my Alpha administers. It's a completely different feeling to what Imre put me through. That gave me no pleasure or arousal whatsoever. That leads me to believe there is some truth to the talk of Alpha and Omega reciprocity.

I should be ashamed of the spectacle I'm making of myself when I throw my head back and shimmy in ecstasy but how can I be embarrassed when he's growling his approval? Of course he doesn't let up with just one orgasm and continues to probe and pinch and twist until I'm loudly groaning out my pleasure again. Punishment and pleasure are definitely both sides of the coin for me.

Antal gives one yank on the rope and my arms drop down, sore from hanging and supporting so much of my weight. He kisses each chafed red wrist, then pushes my upper body down on the mattress while keeping me kneeling. Now I'm totally exposed and he quickly enters me with a happy grunt at my welcoming wetness. He sets a furious pace that soon has me vibrating from the frenzy. Every erogenous zone has been ignited from my whipped behind to my swollen nipples and, especially, my pussy punished inside and out.

His orgasm is accompanied by a long drawn-out howl that I'm sure echoes through the castle. I'm compelled to give voice but by now I'm too hoarse to be loud.

He collapses, his weight pressing down and half-smothering me, but I'm buzzing with contentment. I'm proud that my body can thoroughly satisfy his needs, and give him his own release. Even for his dark urges.

And then he whispers loving words of praise, destroying my post-coital high. I can't bear to be the focus of so much feeling – it's too much. This isn't us. I start to fret and shake as if I'm having an attack of nerves. Why is this happening again?

Antal turns me in his arms so he can see my face but I close my eyes to hide the tears I can't hold back. *Look at me,* he commands and I have to obey so I force myself to blink through the watery veil. He's looking at me like I'm a specimen: he's curious, intrigued, wondering, and confounded.

Then he pulls himself upright and sits me in his lap, straddling him. He just stares into my wet eyes as the tears stream silently down my face. His hands hold on to my sides while his thumbs stroke my nipples but in an absentminded way.

He moves one hand behind my neck while his other fondles both of my breasts. Then Antal leans in as if to kiss – another rare kiss – but I suspect he's just as likely to bite me. He sees that wariness in my face and is delighted before administering a playful nip at my lips then capturing my mouth in a gentle yet passionately persistent kiss.

I'm tingling from the roots of my hair to the soles of my feet as he latches onto my soul and I'm falling, falling, cartwheeling in slow motion in a blaze of white-hot light while time suspends. Pressing his face against mine his cheek is soaked with my tears.

Antal shifts to lay me flat on my stomach and finger-combs the hair up off my neck exposing my nape. He kisses and licks then blows his hot breath which causes me to shiver yet again in arousal and anticipation.

I'm so vulnerable when my neck is bared and my head is bowed to him.

Still my tears keep falling continuously and soundlessly. He turns my head enough to lap at the salty flow, his pleasure evinced in a steady rumble from deep in his chest.

His hands caress up and down my arms a few times before placing them above my head. All the hairs are standing on end from the shivery goosebumps. Now he strokes my sides, catching an edge of breast, until he reaches my hips and thighs.

His hands take hold and lift up my legs, raising my pelvis and turning my bottom right up. It feels painfully tender and no doubt has been welted rosy red. Gently massaging my inner thighs, flesh that received a good portion of the whipping, he compliments my silky-soft skin as his fingers rove all over, ending at my anus. He fondles that hole which seems impossibly tiny for his fingers, never mind his cock, to penetrate.

In my heats he's inserted dildos and butt plugs and taught me to enjoy his dick fucking my ass. But I'm not in heat now and feel a little tense and apprehensive.

Antal is wetting the tip of his cock by moving up and down my soaking slit while stroking himself to generate pre-cum. He smears that over the entrance to my bottom-hole to lubricate me. His cock presses against me, straining to be inside this hot, tight place. He pushes but progress is slow and I'm trembling with the discomfort of this unusual invasion. My hands are clenched into fists and as he enters an inch at a time I pound them on the bed. He pauses with a pained moan but I encourage him to continue saying *yes, yes* because I want to please and pleasure him.

He gives a stronger thrust that takes him deeper. I pant through the pain, breathing loudly. Once he breeches the tight ring of muscle I can force my hips to keep still as Antal impales me. He whispers *szeretlek, szivem (I love you, my heart)* and at those words of devotion my body relaxes enough for him to penetrate fully.

His lengthy sigh of pleasure sends a flood of warmth throughout my being. We hover, motionless, for an eternity that passes in a moment. His hand dives into my pussy searching out my G-spot just as his thumb presses down on my clitoris. I slip out of my conscious mind as I spasm around the languid movements of Antal drawing back then sliding in again and again and again telling me he loves my wet cunt and my tight asshole.

I'm drowning in slick, a slick produced without being in heat. Later I'll think *that's never happened before,* before realizing the powerful emotion of our lovemaking is bringing it on early. I'm not due yet so it won't last but still it's something new. I know a heat is inevitable on this trip but hoped the traveling would delay my natural cycle. This time will be different though, I'm in a place of safety with an Alpha of my own to take care of me, and clan guards to protect me while I nest.

As my body exults in waves of ecstasy I cry out *édesem (darling)* Antal. *Én is szeretlek, (I love you too).*

Eventually, on a hitching breath, I stop crying and murmur that I'm sorry, I don't know what's wrong with me. Antal is unaccustomedly tender with me, holding me in a gentle embrace and lightly kissing my forehead before settling us both for a quick nap.

He never needs to talk dirty during sex because he uses the dirty words all the time calling me his cunt, his slut, his whore who craves his cock. No, what has aroused me, while simultaneously destroyed me, are the sweet loving endearments he murmured in my ear.

I'm not worthy of this man. My own family rejected me. I mean, his did to him but he says they had their reasons. And whether they were right or not at least he knew why.

I know I have changed during the time we've been together, and now I see that Antal has changed too. Emerging from a light doze he tells me his brother, the second son, wants to meet with us. He broods over the idea for a few minutes then giving his head a sharp nod he says to me:

"Yes. You meet Gyuri." Standing to get his phone off the dresser he shows me his magnificent physique, beautifully inked, and classic profile while he rapidly sends off a text. Turning he catches me ogling and that makes him grin. He waves his dick at me asking is the right word hungry or thirsty? *Do you eat my cum or drink it?*

It takes me a moment to interpret that and I laugh out loud once his meaning is clear.

"No, no," I advise, taking an exaggeratedly deep breath, "I inhale it."

And of course he wants a demonstration but warns we have to be quick. So he fucks my mouth hard and I work my lips and tongue inside and my fingers outside until he explodes.

His dick fills me, stretching my lips around his girth, and he presses my face tight against his hard belly so I can't breathe but I can swallow. I've almost blacked out by time he finishes unloading. Pulling out Antal watches me gasp for air with tears once again streaming down my very red face. He reaches between my legs and rumbles his wordless approval when he feels my wetness. This form of sexual asphyxiation turns me on just as much as him choking me.

Saying we have no time he refuses to give me an orgasm and when I whine he asks if I'd like my pussy spanked again to further add to my discomfort. I'm so horny I give the idea serious thought but he simply drags me out of bed saying *No time!* because I have to get cleaned up and dressed before Gyuri arrives.

4

Surprisingly, Gyuri is a homely man. I mean, he's neither attractive nor unattractive, he just looks like a normal guy. There's enough of a resemblance to show he's Antal's relative, but that's where the similarities end. The way he laughs, the shape of his mouth, the color of his eyes are all familiar yet different.

Antal truly is drop-dead gorgeous. I think I sometimes conveniently forget that so I don't add to my own insecure feelings of inadequacy.

The real difference between the brothers is that Gyuri is a happy, calm, and friendly man. After only five minutes in his company I feel like we've been friends for a long time. That's just the way he is.

Even Antal is smiling and relaxing a bit in his older brother's company. He stretches his arm along the back of the love-seat we're in and lets his hand rest lightly on my shoulder. Gyuri notices the gesture, he's sharp, and the smile he gives me is so warm I'm sure he's signaling his approval.

It's too much of a struggle to follow along with their conversation and that's fine, I sit quietly enjoying the cadence of their voices. I'm sure they're talking about people I don't know anyhow, like other family members, friends and neighbors, Gyuri's children, but I don't feel rudely ignored. Actually, I'm experiencing a feeling of camaraderie.

Antal's hand slips around my upper arm and he snugs me closer. I'm struck by the realization that we're presenting as a happy couple and... that is what we are, even if our happiness stems from unusual practices.

After awhile Kartal comes in, greets everyone and slips on to an ottoman beside me so he can translate quietly. It seems Gyuri misses Antal but isn't pressing him to stay in Hungary saying their pack isn't a contented one.

The blame is placed on the fact that Kada and Beata have no children. When the time comes leadership will fall to Gyuri or, by that time it might be his eldest son who takes charge. Gyuri keeps a separate household since he thinks the Szémozsa family home has developed a sad and sour atmosphere and he doesn't want his children growing up in that.

Both Csilla and Sandor come in to say hello and urge Gyuri to stay for a meal but he pleads a prior engagement. It's obvious they're all good friends and comfortable in each other's company. After Gyuri has left Csilla explains to me that unfortunately the same can't be said for the oldest Szémozsa brother or his wife.

"The marriages of lots of pack leaders are respectful rather than loving. That's a common thing since they're more often based on strategic alliances than romantic ideals. But there's a real bitterness between Kada and Beata that you can't help but feel whenever they're around.

We never invite them here for get-togethers, but we do sometimes meet them out at social functions. Although they rarely attend such events. I should feel sorry for them but it's hard since neither one is a sympathetic character."

I don't know how to respond to this so I say nothing. Kartal comes to my rescue by asking Sandor if he thinks Kada and Gyuri will join us in the fight against the Fehers.

Kartal has surprised everyone with his raging determination to avenge and fight for the pack. Because he's a Beta in servitude to his Alpha it's easy to dismiss him but Kartal is a big strong man with fierceness and passion just below the surface.

I've been happy to have him join Antal and me in several of our rough fucking sessions and during my heat. He's taken quite a few of the bites and blows that were aimed my way. Kartal also proved to have a strong arm when wielding the riding whip. This gives Antal greater satisfaction because Kartal can hit him so much harder than I can. Afterwards the three of us collapse on the floor squashed into the shower, soaping and soothing each other's red marks, welts and swellings, bruises, and bloodied bits.

Kartal makes a good temporary replacement for Grigor who had to remain back in America to oversee and protect our home there.

5

"Csilla, I am bored to tears!" declares Erzsébet walking into the sitting-room where Tó has been looking at photos of Csilla and Sandor's children. The mother is sad to be parted from her little ones but it's too dangerous for them to be at home right now. Tó sympathizes and hopes her attempt to show an interest is believable.

"Well, we could have drinks in the garden or play cards or go for a drive if you like," Csilla suggests like a good hostess.

"Yes to drinks and cards but later on. We'll wait until the men finish their business meeting and see if we can't get a couple of tables going. Meanwhile a drive sounds good so long as it ends up in the city and we can do some shopping. What do you think, does that sound good?"

"Shopping? Always! Have the men started their meeting already?"

"I don't think so, Janos was still in our room looking for something on his laptop when I left--"

Csilla immediately stands and taking Tó by the arm says: "We'd better hurry to catch Antal before the meeting starts."

When Tó gives her a quizzical look Csilla asks: "Do you have any money?" and now Tó understands.

The three women go straight to the room Sandor has established for meetings and arrive in time to stop Kartal from closing the door.

Slipping past him Csilla calls out: "Apologies, husband, but I need to check something with Antal," She then turns to him asking: "We're going shopping so do you want to give Tó a credit card? or should I just charge everything and you can settle with Sandor later?"

Antal looks from one woman to the other, frowning, before he flatly states: "Tó can't leave."

"She's not leaving, Antal, she's coming with us. We're going in to the city to shop so hand over your card." Erzsébet speaks impatiently and her husband chuckles, adding:

"Don't bother to argue, Antal. When it comes to shopping the ladies always win."

"That's right. Don't be cheap Antal, just give Tó your card and we'll let you get on with your meeting."

Antal steps forwards crowding the woman as he retorts: "No, Erzsébet. Tó does not go anywhere without me."

Erzsébet gets right in his face demanding: "Why not? Is she your prisoner? Hmm?"

"It's okay, I'll stay here," interjects Tó, but then Sandor intervenes.

"There's no need to be concerned about Tó's safety, Antal. Csilla's always accompanied by her guards and even her driver is armed. The women will be perfectly safe."

Antal growls in frustration before snapping: "I said no."

"Hey, you're not in America now. Maybe she's your captive there but not here, not with us."

Janos was right when he told Antal not to interfere with the shopping trip, his wife is a firebrand. But Antal isn't listening to Erzsébet. He turns to Tó and in English warns her not to go anywhere without him.

Speaking in a placating tone Csilla gently rests her hand on Antal's arm and asks, "What is your concern, Antal? Tó will be safe from the Fehers but is there something else? something about her being out in public that worries you?"

He's still agitated but answers in a normal voice: "Yes."

"Is it... is it something to do with her being recognized?"

"No!"

"Antal, her eyes... you know there was talk and speculation the other night. Who is her family?"

"Tó doesn't know, no one does. It doesn't matter, Tó is staying here."

Erzsébet exchanges a shocked look with her husband and Janos says: "Antal, do you really think Tó is connected to––"

"No, I don't, but as Csilla said there's been speculation. I don't want any rumors getting out about her. She wouldn't be safe."

"But that's absolutely––"

"No, Erzsébet," interrupts Csilla. "Antal is right not to take chances. Tó is a foreigner here and it's best to avoid any trouble."

"Csilla, I know we discussed this before but you don't really suspect that... I mean they've always been very straitlaced, there's never been any talk about illegitimate... well—" Sandor trails off.

Antal replies: "No, the gossip about them always revolves around people dying and disappearing. They're a vicious family and I don't believe Tó is any relation to them, but if they get a hint of scandal they won't hesitate to harm her. Tó stays here where she's safe."

They all look at one other and Tó declares: "Csilla, you and Erzsébet go shopping. I'll settle for that drink in the garden with my eReader. I might even nap a little. I'm not sure what you all are talking about but it doesn't matter, if Antal wants me to stay here then I'm staying."

Erzsébet scowls saying they shouldn't have said anything and just gone out, but Tó smiles at everyone enjoying the warmth of Antal's quick kiss and whispered *jó kislány (good girl)*. Then he heads back into the meeting room confident his wishes will be obeyed.

"We don't have go either--" begins Csilla but Tó insists. Erzsébet tells Csilla she wants to discuss the speculation so they leave the men to their business.

Tó is already settled in a lawn chair with her book when the two older women stop to say goodbye before heading into the city and its stores.

When the morning meeting is over Antal comes outside and finds her napping. Sitting on the grass beside Tó's chair he rests his head in her lap. Waking, she runs her fingers through his hair to lightly scratch and massage his scalp until she can feel him relax.

"All this talk, and making plans, and arguing about who is doing what or going where, is frustrating. I want this business with the Fehers over so we can go home," he grumbles.

"It sounds like there will be a raid or something?"

"Hmm, something like that." His tone is dismissive but Tó is anxious for his safety.

"Antal, you will be careful, right? I know you have to fight, hell I know you *want* to fight, you love it, but don't die and leave me stranded here in Hungary, okay?"

He chuckles at her comment, appreciating the lack of sentimentality, then stands and pulling her out of the lawn chair switches places and lifts her onto his lap. "I will enjoy the fight and I will not die. I will come back covered in the blood of my enemies to ravish you as a victor and protector."

"Oooh, my hero," she teases. "So the wives and I will be safely tucked up in the castle waiting for you men to come back and mess us up?"

"No, not the wives, they'll be fighting too."

"Really? Erzsébet and *Csilla*? in a battle?"

"They're both Alphas and all Alphas will fight, they'll want to. Remember, Csilla has been separated from her children - who were put at terrible risk - so she's angry and vengeful. Erzsébet just likes to fight anyone at any time," he adds with a laugh.

"So are they trained shooters or—-"

"No, no, the women must shift. They can only join the battle in wolf form. That way they're stronger and faster, and better able to slip in and out unseen."

"Antal, I could do that too," Tó says excitedly.

"No, Tó. You're an Omega, even if you weren't raised as one. You cannot join this fight or any other. Unless you're attacked, that is."

"That's not fair!" she retorts.

Antal pauses for a moment, considering her words, before replying: "No, it probably isn't. After all, you've been victimized too, but that makes no difference."

Tó can tell by the way his voice hardens that there's no room for argument. It occurs to her that the frenzy of battle and scent of blood could fully trigger her heat which would be completely disastrous in the midst of an army of Alpha warriors. She shudders at the thought and Antal tightens his arms around her.

6

"Tó is so beautiful I should be terribly jealous that you bedded her, husband."

"Only because she went into heat and I'm an Alpha. If you had been there, my love, I would have ravished you and you know that's true."

Csilla gives Sandor a quick kiss before continuing: "The only reason I'm not jealous is because it's obvious she's absolutely smitten with Antal."

"Yes I see that and frankly it's what makes her beautiful now. She wasn't back then, you know."

"What do you mean?"

"Well she was this wan, washed-out, skinny little kitchen-maid. They had dressed her up in the Club uniform that was practically falling off because she had no curves. Even her beautiful eyes weren't enough to overcome the drabness. The only thing going for her was an incredibly sweet-smelling slick that pulled us in."

"So what happened to cause such a dramatic change?"

"Well, she is very young so getting proper food and rest has let her natural beauty come through, I guess."

"Those eyes and that platinum hair makes me wonder if..."

"Let's not speculate, my dear one."

"No, you're right, we'd better not. But that hair and her slender figure make her look ethereal, angelic, which is such a contrast to Antal who we all know is truly a devil."

"Antal is a psychopath," replies Sandor bluntly.

"Then it's a good thing he's on our side in this war with the Fehers," says his wife.

"Ah, if only it was a war," chimes in Erzsébet arriving for dinner. "If only declarations could be made, lines drawn, sides chosen... instead we have sniping forays and sneaking spies. There's no battle!"

"My bloodthirsty mate," croons Janos, as he comes in with Antal. He lifts his wife's hand to his lips with a gallant flourish before greeting Csilla and Sandor. "And where's your *kis lány (little girl)*, Antal?"

The youngest of the three men narrows his eyes as he looks around the dining-room. "Late!" he hisses and the women shudder at the promised threat in his tone.

After a round of drinks Antal insists everyone sit down to their meal while he rousts Tó from whatever distraction makes her so rudely lose track of time.

"Maybe she fell asleep?" suggests Csilla.

"Probably has her nose in a book – as usual!" Antal replies as he hurries from the room.

Csilla and Erzsébet exchange knowing looks and Csilla shivers. At Sandal's inquiry if she's cold she just shakes her head and gives her husband a grateful smile for being the man he is.

The foursome have barely started on their soup course when a manic howl echos throughout the castle. The women jump in their seats and the men feel their hair stand up at the back of their necks. Rushing from the room they meet Antal racing down the stairs yelling:

"They've taken Tó! She's been kidnapped. There was a struggle and there's blood I know it's hers by the taste, and I can smell chloroform."

Everyone hurries up to Antal and Tó's suite to see the evidence for themselves and to search for clues. Sandor has already received a call from the castle's security detail.

"See, she'd changed her clothes for dinner and look, she'd left the room and was coming downstairs," announces Csilla,

Janos interjects excitedly, pointing at the wall, "There's a smear of blood here and it looks too high up to be from Tó, maybe it's from one of the abductors?"

Antal sniffs at the stain and his jaw clenches as he shakes his head:

"No, that's Tó's blood. Someone has thrown her over their shoulder and didn't care if her head hit the wall."

They can all hear from his voice that he's seething with anger and the wild-eyed gaze he turns on them is filled with blood lust.

Just then Janos, who was bent over studying the rest of the wall in the passageway, straightens up with a jerk asking: "Is Tó in heat?"

"Fuck yes, maybe. She had an episode and went into pre-heat today but a bad scare might have accelerated everything... why? Can you scent her?"

"Faintly but, well, it's still unmistakable..." Antal bends down to join Janos sniffing along the wall and nods his confirmation.

"Oh God! And she's been captured by humans!" moans Csilla.

"We've got to find her right away, what can we do?" demands Erzsébet.

Finishing his call Sandor tells the group to follow him to the surveillance room where there's video footage to see.

"They just watched?" asks Erzsébet, incredulously.

"No, no, one phoned me right away and two more have gone in pursuit. But they've also informed me that we have spies planted in the Feher household and head office and they'll get word to us as soon as they can."

When they arrive in the small security office the video is rolled back and ready to play. Csilla gasps and Antal growls as they watch Tó's valiant attempt to fight off her masked assailants, jerking her head from side to side to avoid a cloth one of them is trying to press to her face. No doubt it's a chloroform-soaked cloth and she would have detected that odor right away.

When her body quivers into shifting mode the biggest man slams his fist into her face sending a spray of blood out of her nose. From the way her head falls back they can see she's lost consciousness.

"He's a dead man," seethes Antal through gritted teeth.

The assailant hoists Tó over his shoulder and when he turns down the corridor her face bangs hard against the wall.

"He will die slowly,"

"Damn!" cried Sandor, looking at his phone. "The guards in pursuit lost them but they were headed in the direction of the Feher family compound. It's gated and secured but we have a woman already in place on the inside."

Antal shifts and the huge dark gray wolf just snaps its teeth before running away.

7

"Milady no! Stay away from this unnatural creature, it shouldn't be allowed to soil your air with its presence. What were they thinking of bringing it here?"

Ladiszla speaks with the familiarity of an old family retainer but she's actually worked for the Fehers less than six months. Still, the middle-aged woman with the strong opinions she vocalizes freely is granted plenty of leeway since she's an excellent cook, a good worker, and has both the family and the rest of the staff intimidated.

Tó is slowly coming into consciousness with her head pounding and she wishes this woman with her loud voice, screeching and complaining, would just shut up.

"This vermin should be in the cellar or the garage, not anywhere near you milady," Ladiszla asserts. "I will force it outside now where it belongs and–"

"Oh wait, Ladiszla, please. I've been told she is the... the, uh... *mate* of Antal Szémozsa, and he's an aristocrat staying in the castle of Sandor Koczinyi, a minor princeling. Surely we must treat this woman with courtesy and respect–"

"No! No! A thousand times no! It isn't even a real woman, it's a mongrel and vicious with it. It should be kept far away from a civilized gentlewoman like yourself, milady. Please, let me take it away now. It makes me sick to my stomach to see it in the same room as you."

And, as usually happens, Ladiszla gets her way and grabbing hold of Tó's ankle drags her out of the room, muttering words like smelly, disgusting, filthy animal.

She keeps up the tirade until they're well out of sight from the house and then the woman pulls Tó to her feet hissing at her: "Shush and just listen to me. I work for Sandor. He had me apply for a job here months ago so I could report back on any threats. No one expected them to grab you nor anyone else. It's all the fault of that Mór he's such a hothead. Thinks he knows better than everybody so he won't listen to anyone's advice."

Tó struggles to waken but shaking her head only makes it hurt more. Her vision is still blurry but she does her best to focus on the older woman and what she's saying.

"Ach, you're still mostly out of it but do you understand enough to just play along and I'll get you out of here tonight." With that she prods Tó towards a cement structure that turns out to be a garage, making a big show of prodding and pushing. Before crossing the threshold Tó turns her head and vomits, nearly hitting Ladiszla's shoe. The woman screeches and shoves Tó through the doorway, slamming the door shut and padlocking it on the outside.

Very little light gets into the garage which helps with Tó's sore head. She finds a corner near the door and curls up on the cement floor. It's cold but she's wearing the long dress she'd changed into for dinner and can wrap the skirt around her legs. Plus, she's got on a t-shirt of Antal's underneath and is wearing it like a slip. She put it on to comfort her with his scent while she was in pre-heat. Ignoring the chill she does manage to drift off.

Tó has been awake for some time, ears strained to listen for the sound of approaching footsteps. Despite being older and thickset Ladiszla is surprisingly light on her feet. Tó hears the woman just before she opens the side door into the garage.

"I thought they'd never finish their dinner. Well, they finished but they wouldn't get up from the table, they were all too busy arguing and yelling. I felt like yelling myself! Oh, I forgot, here's a couple of rolls with meat. Eat up before you go.

Most of the family want to return you immediately but they won't, ach maybe they can't, stand up to Mór. I don't blame them, he's a crazy man. So there's a great uproar in the house. That's why I'm so late, and I'm sorry about it, I'm sorry for myself too because I've decided I've got to leave now as well and I'm too old to be staying up all hours."

Tó is thankful that last sleep took care of her headache because Ladislza's constant chatter is annoying, but at least she speaks English and she's on Tó's side.

"Anyhow, here's what's going to happen. I'm going to give you my phone to take and some cash as well. You'll travel directly from the back of the garage, across the lawns – that's the riskiest part – and then go through the bit of woods that you'll come to which will get you to the edge of the Feher property line. Got that so far?"

Tó nods and Ladiszla continues with her instructions.

"If you keep following the fence you'll come to a service road, it's what the workmen and delivery trucks use. You can get off the property there. There's a night watchman who will probably be asleep because there's almost never any traffic along there when it's late but be quiet just in case.

The service road goes into town but long before then you'll come to a gas station with a 24-hour convenience store. From there you can call the castle, then go inside and have a coffee or a cold drink while you wait to get picked up. I'm going to send a text to Sandor telling him you're free now, but working your way off the property and you'll call when you reach the pick-up spot."

Tó impatiently bites down on her lip while the woman's bent old fingers laboriously type out the message. Which she's probably writing in Hungarian, thinks Tó, and the keyboard probably uses the Cyrillic alphabet. She forces herself to be patient. Finally the message is sent and the woman shows Tó that Sandor's number is right at the top so she can call him easily.

Tó's been gone for about seven hours and her body aches for her Alpha. She doesn't even know if she has a wave but sends out a call anyhow, hoping he might be able to pick up her weak signal.

She feels stronger now that her head has cleared and she's determined to safely get free from the Feher compound. Her need to be with Antal gives her confidence.

8

The local wolf clans all arrive at the castle to plan out their counter-attack on the Fehers. The men prevented Antal from leaving in his wolf form and argued him into shifting back. But now he's refusing to meet with anyone, he is enraged at the inactivity and just wants to go. He's scented Tó's heat in the hallway and is suffering a ferocious need to find his mate and rut.

His brothers do force him to stay and have a few words with them. They all listen to the update Sandor's had from Ladiszla. Now that they know Tó is no longer captive they decide to attack the property.

"We should negotiate with the Fehers--" begins Sandor.

Janos interrupts arguing: "No! now is the time to wipe out those *baszós (fuckers)*, that gang of humans, while we're all together and acting as one."

"But they have women and children at the compound!"

"Husband, they showed no mercy to our children when they set off that bomb at the school," declares Csilla.

Antal tells them he'll burn everything down and, since he doesn't plan to stay in, or ever return to, Hungary they can lay the blame on him. He doesn't wait for further discussion, just grabs Kartal and orders him to drive.

The Feher compound is huge. It's gated with guards patrolling inside the fence. Their dogs start snarling as they detect the smell of the shifters.

"We need to wait for everyone to arrive, we need lots of fuel. I'll text them to make sure they're all loaded up," says Kartal. He's eager to begin but realizes just the two of them can't make any kind of an impact.

"I'm going to prowl the perimeter to see if I can get a lead on Tó. If I do I will go after her so don't wait for me," Antal tells him, quickly stripping out of his clothes and shifting. His senses are sharper when he's in his wolf form. The leashed dogs start barking like mad and Antal snarls at them, making the guards strain to see through the darkness. They know the dogs sense a presence.

The big gray wolf lopes off and soon he's trotting through the woods. He thinks he can hear a faint wafted cry from Tó but wonders if that's just his hopeful imagination. *No of course it isn't,* Antal tells himself, *I have no imagination.*

After circling about halfway through the woods he arrives at the service road and picks up Tó's scent. He throws back his head and from the depths of his belly he looses a hair-raising howl to call to his mate.

Tó escapes from the Feher property and successfully makes her way along the road until she spots the lights for the gas station. It's been a long, tiring hike in human form but she can't shift because she needs to carry the phone and the money and wear clothes. Her dress doesn't have pockets.

Unfortunately her arrival at the gas station is greeted by several loitering youths bored and looking for trouble. *America or Hungary, it's always the same with adolescents* she thinks with a sigh.

The young men immediately surround and grab at her. Tó ducks and dodges and avoids capture but they manage to take her phone and the cash she's carrying in her hand.

The store clerk is secluded in a booth and refuses to come out to help but Tó remembers the Hungarian word for police, *rendőrség*, and screams at him to call. She slips free from the boys and races to the door of the convenience store, escaping the men by a hairs-breadth, before locking it behind her. The clerk nods vigorously holding up his phone to show the gang of boys that he has called. They run away from the threat of the law.

Tó speaks very little of the language, and doesn't know if the clerk really has called the authorities, but knows she can't be around when they arrive. She's tired out now, her body still feeling the after-effects of the chloroform, and she's struggling to think straight and figure out a plan. Although the headache is long gone her mind feels fuzzy, but that might just be her pre-heat.

Even if she could borrow the clerk's phone she has no idea what number to call. With no means of communication or travel Tó has no choice but to shift. Normally that wouldn't be a problem but being in wolf form makes it much harder to suppress her heat. Her animal wants to obey its natural urges, and now that she has an Alpha she is compelled to find him. Her senses are heightened and she's listening carefully to hear his mating call.

She leaves the store and as soon as she's out of the clerk's sight she shifts and heads back towards the Feher estate.

Ladiszla said she'd be getting out tonight as well, wanting to be miles away before there's any retaliation. Tó hopes she can meet up with the woman or pick up enough of her scent to follow. In her wolf form she moves much more quickly and is soon nearing the estate when she hears her Alpha's howl. Tó starts to run. Soon she sees the flames rising up behind the trees, hears the crackle of a hungry fire, and feels a wall of heat.

Antal is racing alongside the road, more comfortable in the grassy sward leading to the forested area. He hears a car approaching from behind but isn't concerned about being seen, his coloring blends well with the moonlit night. Besides, he's sure the driver will be intent on escaping the burning buildings.

Tó is in the middle road when the car catches sight of her silvery coat in its headlights. She just stands there, disoriented from brain fog now she's fully in heat.

Instead of swerving round her the car skids to a halt and Mór Feher jumps out brandishing a rifle which he quickly hoists up to his shoulder.

"*Farkas (wolf)*," he hisses, rage lighting his eyes in a blaze of madness. He takes aim with his gun but Antal leaps through the air growling ferociously. Startled, Mór's shot goes wide and in a moment the big dark gray beast knocks him to the ground and is tearing through the back of his neck to get at his throat.

Tó races to her protector and whines at him. With Mór dead, his hot blood staining Antal's muzzle, the Alpha is free to take his Omega. Tó drops her forelegs raising her haunches while Antal mounts her with a furious passion. He bites her shoulders while she yips encouragement. Their rutting is noisy, nasty, vicious, and oh-so satisfying to both animals.

Soon another car drives up slowly, stopping behind Mór's abandoned vehicle. It's Kartal with ash on his face and his body stinking of gasoline, come to their rescue.

He's got Antal's clothes in the car. The wolves shift back to human form and Antal puts on his pants while handing Tó his shirt. Before she can slip into it Kartal, fired up from the night's events, turns to Antal with a wide grin and gets the Alpha's permission to ravage the Omega in heat.

Tó welcomes Kartal's attentions, tilting her pussy up to him, but turns her face to Antal, licking her lips in invitation. Antal feeds her his cock and she takes him deep while being roughly fucked by Kartal from behind. Her sweet scent wafts over both men, increasing everyone's desire and pleasure. After both men orgasm, once to Tó's three times, they collapse in a sweaty heap. Kartal breaks away first, leaving Tó securely held in her Alpha's tender embrace.

She turns to Antal saying: "Now that you've killed my assassin we're even, we're equals."

He chuckles and tells her she's crazy and *aranyos (adorable)*. Tó doesn't bother to argue, her body has already noticed that Antal's refractory period has waned and he's hard for her again.

He pulls Tó into the back-seat of Kartal's car and she straddles him. She's put on his shirt but he makes her leave it open so he can enjoy the jiggle of her small breasts while she bounces on his cock. He twists her swollen nipples and gives a rumbling growl. She purrs in response and Kartal smiles as he drives them home.

"Kartal wait! Stop the car!" Tó cries out. Taking Antal's face in her hands she stares earnestly into his eyes asking: "Can we shift and run through the woods together?"

"What, now? You'd like that?"

"I'd love that. It's dark and scary but it was scarier when I was kidnapped and thought I'd never see you again. I would hate to die without ever having been chased by you, the smell of my slick driving you mad with lust as you race after me. Will you chase me, Alpha?"

Antal growls with pleasure, giving her the order to *Run, Omega!* and Tó shifts and flees.

Leaning over the back of his seat Kartal says it will take him about forty-five minutes to an hour to deal with the clean-up and will that be enough time?

"Yes, Tó has never been in the hunt before so I'm sure I'll catch her quickly. You go ahead and do the necessary and we'll meet back here."

Kartal nods and watches Antal shift into his big Alpha wolf form. Then he drives back the way they came so he can arrange Mór Feher's body in a way that disguises how he died.

He has to leave the corpse behind so the Fehers know he hasn't been kidnapped which would necessitate more fighting. Except they'll be in no position to fight, not with their compound destroyed by the fire. He hopes this will signal the end of the Fehers in this territory.

Then he sighs at the thought of chasing a she-wolf of his own through the woods in the dark of night, and the delightful pleasure when she's captured.

9

Fast-moving clouds pass over the moon at intervals but there's still plenty of light for wolves to see by. Tó is so excited she's trembling in the exhilaration of racing through the trees in the dark.

Her wolf is sure-footed leaping over tree roots and the small, scrubby plants that cover the forest floor. Her pale fur will draw Antal like a beacon but so long as she runs as swiftly as she can she'll be satisfied with her first-time performance.

Besides, she wants to be caught and fucked by the victor, her Alpha.

Tó flees, listening intently for the expected sound of Antal crashing behind her as he closes in, so she's shocked when his wolf suddenly tackles her to the ground. He's a silent and stealthy stalking predator who has captured his prey and pinned her beneath his weight.

The two animals are panting from their run and now wrestle playfully before Antal grabs Tó in his powerful jaws and shakes her into position so he can claim his win with quick, rough sex. Her surrender isn't graceful but her lusty appetite makes up for it.

It's decades since Antal has run with a pack, not since his youth, and he resolves to start up the practice again with his entourage at home. Tó catches his eye and they share the same thought. They will do this again and again.

Happily the wolves trot back to the spot where Kartal is just finishing the clean up of their earlier kill.

10

Back on American soil the tired couple deplane into the care of Grigor who is waiting with the car. Tó was unable to sleep on the plane although she handled the flight better this time.

She's dozing in the car on the drive home while Antal shares news of their relatives in the Szémozsa family. He and Grigor speak far too quickly for Tó to keep up but Antal's voice grows cold when he speaks of Imre, and Grigor's voice is angry when he hears about Stefan. Tó has suspected for some time now that Grigor's feelings towards his Alpha run very deep.

It reminds her that she never did ask Antal about his history with the mouth-watering Stefan. She suspects it was the sexual exploration of two youths and maybe Stefan never moved on? He certainly wasn't interested in meeting Tó, and he'd looked at her with disdain.

Arriving home they're confronted with a Lamborghini Aventador in the driveway. A slender but muscular blond of medium height is lounging against the red car.

"Alpha," whispers Grigor in awe. "That's $400,000 worth of sportscar."

"At least that much," replied Antal nudging Tó until she's wide awake. Grigor hurries around to open their door and as he does so the young man straightens up and removes his sunglasses. Grigor immediately falls to his knees, head bowed and murmuring *your Majesty*.

Tó steps out of the car and lifting her head freezes in shock. She sees aquamarine eyes in a face that looks very much like her own. The young man nods, greeting her: "Lake. Sister."

She remains stuck staring for a long moment before drawing a shaky breath and turning to Antal commands: "Kill him."

Antal kicks Grigor telling him to stand up, that the Royalty of Europe has no authority here.

"Lake! What are you saying? Why do you want this man to kill me, your twin?"

"My twin? You're telling me you're my brother? In that case, I'm just returning the favor."

The Beta stands, but casts the newcomer an apologetic look. He knows the man is Prince River, a descendant of the House of Jagiellon from its second reign. A true blue-blooded Royal.

Grigor realizes Antal isn't surprised, his Alpha must have known about the relationship. Known or suspected. Grigor isn't quite clear about what exactly all of this means... *Oh God*, he thinks, *what if I've fucked the mouth of a Princess? and made her swallow, too!*

"It was hardly my decision since I was only a babe as well!" Prince River retorts.

Leaning towards him aggressively Tó hisses: "That was only true the first time my loving family tried to kill me. You were totally onboard seven years ago!"

"I was completely under our parent's thumb, only thirteen–"

"Fourteen."

"Okay, fourteen years old, big deal. They made all of the decisions for the family and particularly for me. You triggered something when you started digging for your birth certificate, and at the worst possible time.

Our parents said you were dead so they were negotiating a deal with me and our cousin Breeze. And if that hadn't worked out there was still Zephyr."

"I have no idea who you're talking about," yells Tó.

She is visibly agitated so Antal takes charge by inviting Prince River to come into the house for a private discussion. The prince signals to his men, standing unobtrusively beyond the driveway, and the group heads inside.

Once there Antal dispatches Grigor for refreshments, telling him to take the bodyguards to the kitchen. They dispute the order but obey after a sharp command from their prince.

Prince River then turns to Tó explaining: "Your cousins. Look, you know it's our custom to marry our siblings and if there is no brother or sister then we marry our cousins."

"No, I don't know anything about what you or your family do."

"They're your family too, Lake."

"Hardly. I might be their blood but they disowned me at birth although I have no idea why. Besides, Grigor called you *Prince* and I'm not Royalty."

"But of course you are. You are my sister, my twin, and will be my Queen Consort."

"Uh, hard pass on that. One, I call bullshit and two, not interested."

"We explained that when we met up with you–"

"No, no one explained anything. What I heard were snarls, you were all wolves, so I only got a mixed-up jumble of angry thoughts using foreign words. Plus a few nasty remarks muttered about me being the runt of the litter, weak and sickly, polluting the bloodline, yadda-yadda but I had no idea what any of that meant. As far as I was concerned you were just a bunch of crazies who were trying to kill me."

"No we weren't, we couldn't, a Royal can't be killed for God's sake, that's treason. Look, it's true you were abandoned but only because they felt you wouldn't be able to produce a healthy heir."

"I was dumped in the street like a dog and whoever did that, I mean my parents obviously..." she pauses, the words choking her. Antal steps close behind her, pulling her against his chest and holding her protectively in the circle of his arms. Tó takes strength from his embrace and continues: "I still don't know who my parents were, but I do know they expected me to die. You said yourself that they told you I was dead."

"I told you, that happened when we were born–"

"If what you say is true – and that's a mega-huge IF – then when we met up again it was *you* who tried to kill me. I remember being terrified and fighting for my life."

Prince River pulls up the sleeve of his cashmere sweater to show an ugly, jagged scar on his forearm.

"I only wanted to capture you, but you got your jaws into me first. I had to get treated for rabies just in case. You were feral, living on the street, raised as a human until you reached adolescence. Our parent's decreed that our people would never accept you–"

"A filthy guttersnipe, that's what one of *your people* called me. But who put me in the gutter?" Tó shakes her head, still angry. "I had to flee for my life. I couldn't finish school and I've only ever worked at menial jobs to hide behind the scenes, trying to stay under the radar.

I've been in hiding and on the run for years and I never knew where the danger came from or why. Now you're telling me it was my so-called family hunting me down. Well then, I want nothing to do with them, and especially nothing to do with you!"

The prince is angry now too and Antal is amused at the sight of two pairs of aquamarine eyes flashing at each other. As brother and sister the two aren't identical twins but the resemblance is amazingly close. That's what everyone was alluding to on their recent Hungarian trip.

Based on her agitation Tó realizes and believes what Prince River is saying, even if she won't accept it, thinks Antal.

"Once the orphanage started making enquiries we had to investigate the possibility that you were still alive. Even that trip you just made to Hungary has gotten people talking and speculating about Princess Lake, wondering where she's been all these years.

Look, I don't want to marry you either but now that you're a healthy adult of marriageable age I've been sent to claim you. I don't have a choice. Do you think I want sullied goods for my wife? I mean, we've heard about you and your uncontrolled heats, fucking every male in your vicinity, and we've been shamed by it–"

Tó interrupts him in a rage screaming: "YOU! It's all about YOU, the favorite, the special one, the spoiled one. Well let me tell you you're *nothing*. You live in a cocoon of wealth under the complete control of my birth units but I am a survivor. I overcame the odds and fought for everything I have. I am not ashamed."

Her eyes are flashing and her color is high. Antal feels so proud of his *csinos farkas (pretty wolf)*, she's not a *kis nyuszi (little bunny)* anymore.

She breaks off then seeing a hint of fear in her brother's eyes. He'll never understand and despite being twins there is absolutely no connection between them.

Recovering his poise he ignores her outburst and continues: "So long as you exist I have to fulfill my duty and marry you–"

"You can't marry Tó because she's already married to me," interjects Antal. He has no idea he's going to say that until the words spill out, yet he's speaking casually as if what he's saying isn't a shocking bombshell.

Brother and sister both turn to him. Tó's expression is stunned while Prince River's is hopeful, but then his eyes narrow in suspicion and he asks:

"We never heard about this and our spies have kept close tabs on her."

"Huh, only to watch, never to help. They would never intervene to save my life when all they wanted was to see it end," states Tó. "I wonder if sometimes the Fehers were blamed for vile acts committed by your people?"

Antal tightens his embrace and directs his implacable stare at the younger man.

"They watch here, maybe, but the wedding only just happened when we were in Hungary. We got married there, with my family, although I suppose we'll need a civil ceremony to make it legal in America, too?" he looks down at Tó as if she'll know the answer.

"But she's not wearing your mark," the prince points out.

"She is, actually, but in a place you'll never see," growls Antal in a tone of voice that's menacing enough to warn the prince to drop the subject.

Prince River doesn't look entirely convinced, but it's obvious he'd like to be.

Antal explains to Tó: "Your brother wants to marry Princess Breeze who is pretty, and whose branch of the family is very wealthy."

Tó looks at her twin and says: "She's welcome to you, then. My husband and I won't be attending the wedding. I've never known my family and I don't want to start now. I have no idea why they abandoned me and I don't want, or need, to know. They rejected me then so now I reject them."

She turns her back to him and tosses a remark over her shoulder before walking away: "In fact, there's no reason for you and I to ever see each other again."

Antal turns to Grigor with an order and Grigor goes to fetch the bodyguards. Moments later, and with nothing more to say, the prince and his entourage are gone.

Antal yanks Tó back towards himself and with a sardonic grin on his face performs a sweeping bow saying: "My princess."

Tó puts her hands on her hips but grins back as she answers: "Fuck off, *husband.*"

Laughing, Antal lifts her up and twirling her around says: "Your brother is happy now that the problem of your existence is settled, and my brothers will be pleased that I, the black sheep, have managed to marry into such an illustrious family."

"What, you mean you really do want to get married?"

"Grigor, marry tomorrow," is Antal's reply and his Beta turns away phoning for arrangements to be made.

"Hmm, that's quite the romantic proposal, Antal," Tó deadpans but he just waves her comment aside.

"Tó, do you know this?" Antal takes out his own phone and pulls up a translation app typing in a Hungarian word. He turns the screen to show her:

Csomózás = Knotting

but she's completely in the dark and just shrugs at him, questioning. His brow creases in confusion and he taps on the screen again as if she's missing something.

"Knotting, yeah I see the word but I don't know why you're showing it to me."

"K-notting," he says.

"No, you don't pronounce the *k*, just say it as *notting*."

He continues to stare like she's being obtuse. Grigor, having finished his business, tries to help saying: "Tó, you know what is? What is knotting?"

He's speaking extra loudly as if that will clarify things.

She just shakes her head and suddenly Antal has landed two sharp swats to her backside, each accompanied by a word: Learn [spank!] Knotting [spank!].

She scowls at him and rubbing her backside refuses his offer of his phone preferring, to use an iPad. They have those devices scattered throughout the house so she doesn't have to go far to get her hands on one. Sitting down Tó opens up the browser and searches for knotting. After getting results for macramé, and Celtic designs, and fishing rope Antal leans over to see and huffs in annoyance.

Tó tries again, this time searching for Knotting + Alpha.

"Oh my fucking God," she says in shock, adding: "It's even got pictures!"

Now Antal has taken over the iPad and shaking his head says *kutya (dog)? no, no farkas (wolf)*!

Tó snatches the device back and swipes past the clinical photos of dogs until she gets to text content. She taps open an article, starts reading, then gives Antal a look of wide-eyed surprise.

She reads out loud: "Knotting is a ritual performed by the Alpha to bond with his Omega. An act that binds the couple with excruciating pain and excruciating pleasure. It can last for hours and is considered to be the ultimate mating experience."

Now he's nodding at her with enthusiasm. "Tó, I have never knotted before, I never felt driven to do it, so this will be new to me, too."

She realizes that knotting provides much more than a sexual connection and is flattered Antal wants to share this experience with her, but she still has reservations.

"Excruciating pain and pleasure? Well, I know from first-hand experience that you're a master at delivering both. But this knotting... it says here that it's also to facilitate CONCEPTION. Seriously?!! I've been getting shots for birth control but I haven't had one since we went to Hungary. Actually, a few weeks before we went and we've been gone for... uh-oh, I've missed at least two shots – maybe three!"

She turns to Antal and make the gesture of rocking a baby in her arms. He immediately understands and chuckling, nods again.

"WHAT THE FUCK !!!!" her mouth has fallen open and she's gaping like a fish but he just smiles. "Oh no, not that, not the killer smile.

No! No-no-no, don't distract me with that panty-melting, libido-off-the-charts smile."

He doesn't understand her words but appreciates the meaning and pulls her close, kissing her lips hard, then soft, then hard again, all the while murmuring loving words in his native language.

Tó has no trouble understanding him when Antal circles his hand around her abdomen.

She takes hold of his hand saying: "I still don't have a belly but at least I'm no longer concave. Now the skin stretches smooth and flat between my hipbones, see? And I'd like to keep it that way."

But as she watches his face while he strokes her she feels the emotion bubble up inside. He meets her eyes and shrugs his shoulders. *Not exactly an enthusiastic endorsement,* she thinks to herself, *which leaves me oddly relieved. I think he means if it happens it happens.*

"Tó what your brother said is true and I need to mark my *feleség (wife)* properly. Go to my room and be waiting, naked, in my bed. Our bed."

Antal's hunger for Tó shows on his dark, handsome face. In return, her aquamarine eyes are sparkling brilliantly as she happily answers:

"Yes, my Alpha."

11

I'm lying on the bed, naked as instructed, waiting for Antal. Between meeting again after all these years with the man I now know to be my hateful brother and being proposed to... well, sort of, it's been an emotional day.

By this time tomorrow I'll be a married woman. I don't think I want to marry Antal but I can't keep the grin off my face so... maybe? Anyhow, I doubt if I have any say in the matter.

When Antal comes in he has an expression that I can't interpret. His usual impassive look never gives any clues to what he's thinking but this is something different. He sits on the side of the bed and lets his hand trail down my body, smiling when my nipples harden and noticing how my skin goosebumps under his fingers. Despite the smile he has a serious look. Not implacable and stern, but a concentration that I haven't seen before.

My Hungarian has improved considerably so I understand him when he says, accompanied by this new solemn look: "Tomorrow we sign papers but tonight you will truly become my wife."

It makes me shiver.

In a mixture of Hungarian and English, because I'm still trying to teach him my language, I ask about the knotting and will it hurt? He tells me that he's heard it will but not for too long. He adds that Janos was jealous to learn Antal is still waiting for his first time, but said that every time is extraordinary.

I guess I'm giving him a puzzled look because he goes on to explain that he meant it when he said he's never done it before. Now I'm sure my face is surprised. I didn't know it was something he could suppress.

202

I thought it was purely physical but now I realize there needs to be a strong emotional connection as well.

Now I'm overwhelmed with a full heart.

He undresses then lies down beside me and we start kissing. Deep, breathe-the-air-from-my-lungs kisses that make me dizzy with longing. His hands are gentle as he pushes my hair off my face, brushes his fingers against my cheek, and strokes my body with light caresses.

I'm caught up in the languid feeling that time has suspended, and when he enters me our lovemaking is exquisite. Even my orgasm is a gentle roll instead of a bucking frenzy. He groans deep in his throat and takes my hand to feel the swelling form at the base of his cock. I'm not sure if it's too sensitive for my touch but he's guided my fingers here so I explore carefully. I feel the knot harden as it moves up his shaft.

He's already filled my entry, my labia stretched round his girth, so it seems impossible that this knot can be passed inside me. He keeps pumping slowly, shifting his hip in a circular motion, and after several moments of really sharp pain that takes my breath away the knot slips in and we are fully sealed. I can't breathe. I need to remain motionless to hold a piercing pain at bay. But in just a moment more the most extraordinary sensation of ecstasy engulfs both of us.

His dark eyes gaze into mine with wonder and I know mine have widened in delight. This is a breathtaking experience for us to share for the first time. It's heavenly, excruciating joy.

In a novel I once read the main character recalls something about *the union of man and woman being a wonder and an astonishment.* Now, for the first time, I understand what that means. All of the sex I've had during my heats is nothing compared to this mind-blowing experience.

Antal leans down and nuzzling my throat, where my neck meets my shoulder, suddenly bites down and I scream with the pain of his teeth and the pleasure of my orgasm. He soothes the bite mark with licks. When he lifts his head to admire it his lips are wet with my blood. He rubs them over my mouth so we both get that salty taste. I nip at his tongue and he growls a mock warning.

We are bonded and I am swooning in the warm safety of his loving embrace. He warns me that later he'll mark my inner thigh – just like he hinted to Prince River that he'd done already.

"I never wanted a wife Tó, but I am happy I got you."

I doze off. I'm not sure how long I sleep but it's awhile because the sky is now full of stars. Nothing like that night we visited the ruined monastery, though. I'll never forget that experience.

Antal has remained quietly on his back, his arms holding my body in place while our knotting holds us meshed together inside. Tomorrow is our wedding day but tonight has been the consummation of our mating.

"Antal, *szeretlek (I love you)*."

"Tó, *szivem (my heart)*."

"Antal is my *gyilkos hős (killer hero)*."

"I am your *Sötét Nagyúr (Dark Lord)*."

I feel a frisson of pleasurable fear at these words of his spoken in such a deep commanding tone. Like a good Omega I cast my gaze down to reply:

"Yes, my husband, my Master, my Alpha!"

Then I lift up my eyes to challenge him with an aquamarine glare and a delighted laughs escapes him. Then he rumbles a promise and a threat and I sigh with contentment.

Epilogue

10 Days Later

Tó is immersed in her book when Antal walks into the room saying: "Tó? I told you to go to bed."

"I *am* in bed," she points out despite knowing she's risking two spanks for arguing.

"You still have your book," he gestures to her eReader. She closes it and puts it on the night-table, turning off the lamp and plugging the device into the charger at its base.

"And you've still got your iPad."

Antal narrows his eyes and she holds her breath while waiting for his mood barometer to swing to raging anger? or pleasantly easy-going? After a pause he taps his chest and declares:

"Me Alpha-hole." and Tó sputters out a surprised – and relieved – laugh.

He tosses the iPad on the bed before quickly stripping off, barely giving her a chance to enjoy the show before he's under the covers and pulling Tó in a cuddle against his chest.

The two of them spent a very pleasant afternoon in the company of Grigor and his Maritsza, everyone naked and enjoying their lover's bodies.

The Beta and his mate will join the sex party when Tó goes into heat but until then only Antal fucks Tó, and she is the only one he is fucking.

Now that I've admitted to myself that I do have feelings for Antal I'm pretty sure I'd hate to see him enjoying another woman, thinks Tó.

Grigor has found himself an excellent mate in Maritsza who clearly adores the big man. Antal is right about Maritsza being fat, but it's clear that in Grigor's eyes she's absolutely perfect.

Tó wonders if Maritsza's compliance is forced after spotting the woman's thoroughly spanked bottom. But Maritsza joins in with such impassioned abandon that Tó is reassured she wasn't coerced.

And Tó got to satisfy her curiosity by squeezing and fondling Maritsza's big breasts. *Soft but firm,* she'd exclaimed then looked down at herself with an expression so woeful that Antal had taken her in his arms to nuzzle, caress, and suck on her nipples declaring them *édes (sweet).*

She is smiling over the memory when he picks up the iPad again and asks: "Do you want to be a princess?"

Pulling away so she can turn and see his face she asks: "No! What are you talking about?"

"Well, it seems that technically you already are the Princess Lake so do you want to be recognized as her?"

"Fuck no, why would you even ask that? Antal, I never dreamed that someday I would be your wife. I'm thrilled with what I've got, with what we've got. Why would I want anything else?"

"Well, it is your birthright—"

"Huh! That family? Hell, no! I mean, they're not even real Royalty, right?"

"Oh their claim, their bloodline, is acknowledged by the Hungarian people, but they don't actually have any power or any say in anything that goes on. They aren't even figureheads, they don't represent us, we're a republic.

The Jagiellon descendants are merely titled wealthy landowners who think themselves superior to the rest of us. I am a princeling myself, though much good does it do me!"

"Why are you even talking about this stuff?"

"Because you, my dear *feleség (wife)*, are a social media sensation."

"What?"

Passing over the iPad Antal says, "See for yourself."

Blog post from *Injustice:*

WHERE IS PRINCESS LAKE?

Why is the Royal Family hiding

The Princess, and where?

Her loyal subjects want to know!

Blog post from *EuroVibes:*

PRINCESS LAKE FOUND???

An unnamed Palace source reports that Princess Lake is now married to Antal Szémozsa, and living with her import/export businessman husband in America.

Her many followers ask *"Why has this Royal been hidden away and denied her birthright?"*

Social Media post gone viral:

SIGN THIS PETITION AND FORWARD:

Give Princess Lake her Royal Rights!

"Oh Antal," Tó exclaims, "This is ridiculous!"

"It's not, look how many people are following this," he says pointing to the numbers indicating *following* and *share*.

"Do they really have a palace?"

"There are a lot of castles in Hungary, princess."

"Ugh, don't call me that. Who could have leaked this news? Surely not my brother?"

"I think it was. Actually I think Erzsebet is behind the original stories, it's the kind of thing she would think is funny, but she would never give out my name. She knows the last thing I want is for the authorities to look too closely at my *import/export business.*"

"Well, I bet my so-called family doesn't think it's funny, I'm sure they hate having this many people give me recognition and call them out demanding an explanation."

Antal squeezes her tight and his voice has grown husky and low as he asks: "That makes you happy, doesn't it?"

Tó slips round in his embrace so she can slide her arms around his neck and draw close for a kiss replying: "Fuck, yeah! Soooo happy."

Also by Lori Laidlaw

About the Author

Lori is a bit shy...

She confesses she's half in love with all of her characters... and their moods range from playful to dangerous and everything in between!

Spicy and steamy but not boringly clinically explicit descriptions. Instead her scenes are designed to stimulate your imagination, with multiple POV stories expressing mature themes and passionate encounters.

Lori's latest publication is a wolf-shifter omegaverse titled "Lockdown + 3 Alphas = Heat: An Omega's THRILLING dark romantic adventure".

Lori recently published "Girlie" taken from her "Girlie and the O'Shea Brothers" 6-part series of novelettes now revised and rewritten into one novel with additional content.

A couple of holiday-themed short stories exploring the DD/lg dynamic: "Santa's Christmas Party with the Littles", and "A New Year's Resolution for Boss Daddy's Tardy Middle".

"Dared to Bare", the story of a married couple's playtime with erotic spanking. It includes six fun and sexy short stories.

Her first novella was "Secrets, Secrets", a new adult RH dabble.

Read more at https://lori-laidlaw-novelist-bvwonn.mailerpage.io/.